A SAVAGE
DECEPTION

A GUARDIANS OF THE BONES NOVEL

K.J. JACKSON

First Edition: February 2023
ISBN: 978-1-940149-79-0

K.J. Jackson Books

Historical Romance:

Hold Your Breath
Stone Devil Duke
Unmasking the Marquess
My Captain, My Earl

Lords of Fate
Worth of a Duke
Earl of Destiny
Marquess of Fortune

Lords of Action
Vow
Promise
Oath

Revelry's Tempest
Of Valor & Vice
Of Sin & Sanctuary
Of Risk & Redemption
To Capture a Rogue, *Logan's Legends*
To Capture a Warrior, *Logan's Legends*

The Devil in the Duke

Valor of Vinehill
The Iron Earl
The Wolf Duke
The Steel Rogue
The Christmas Countess
The Devil Baron

Box of Draupnir
The Heart of an Earl
The Blood of a Baron
The Soul of a Rogue

Exile
Exiled Duke
Wicked Exile
Dangerous Exile

Guardians of the Bones
Discreet Destruction
Shadows of Scandal
A Savage Deception

Paranormal Romance:
Flame Moon
Triple Infinity, *Flame Moon #2*
Flux Flame, *Flame Moon #3*

Contemporary Romance:
A Beautiful Average

Be sure to sign up for news of my next releases at
www.KJJackson.com

DEDICATION

– As Always,
For my favorite Ks

{ PROLOGUE }

He found her in the bowels of the building.

Crying.

He could hear her tears even as he stepped down the stairs, his feet light, his skill at silent footfalls so ingrained that he walked covertly even when he didn't need to.

His steps could be heavy, loud, here at the main building of the Guardians of the Bones. He could be himself, but he'd found it hard to switch back and forth at this point. To be one person one minute. Another the next.

All necessary for his job as a covert guard for hire, but he hadn't been himself in a long while.

At the bottom of the stairs, he stopped, his head cocking to the side to follow the sound.

To the right.

To the servants' table that would be empty at this time of night.

He hadn't taken even a step into the room with the wide rough-hewn table and thick stone walls before Josie turned her head to him. She could hear anything. Even his silent steps. Even when she was crying.

"Silas." Her eyes were red, swollen like someone had landed not just one blow on her but two. That would be unusual, for Josie was nothing if not quick and agile. One blow maybe. Not two.

She swiped her fingers across her wet cheeks.

"Josie, what is this? If it's tears about the news Hector had, there is no need for them. You know what this will mean for us—both of us?" He moved fully into the room, stopping in front of her sitting on the end of the long bench that flanked the table. Even though they were below ground, the cinnamon that cook always had simmering filled the room, somehow taking the dankness out of the space.

His fingers unconsciously went to her dark brown hair, the color so rich one would swear there was a nighttime rainbow glowing under the darkness, and he slid back the strands that had fallen from her chignon.

He hadn't seen her with her hair askew in a long time.

"I would have thought you'd be waiting for me with champagne and a smile on your face with the news. Not this."

A crushing smile twisted her lips as she pulled away from his hand. "No. It isn't that. The title—that is good news. I'm happy he chose you, especially as Leander was a contender."

Silas stared down at the crown of her head, for her gaze had dropped to his shoes. "Then what is this about?"

Long seconds passed and his pulse started to quicken. Something was wrong—terribly wrong.

She finally lifted her chin to look up at him. "My father is coming back. He'll arrive in a month."

Instant fury kicked into his chest, so thick it had nowhere to go but to crawl up his throat, choking him.

She expelled a shaky sigh, her fingers rubbing against her brow. "And you know what he will do."

"He doesn't know where you are."

"He'll find me. He always does."

His anger spun into full-on rage and he couldn't force air into his lungs, much less force a breath out enough to speak. A snarl curled his lips as he choked out words. "I won't let it happen."

Her big brown eyes looked up to him. Eyes that held everything that was good and right in this world. "You can't do anything to stop it, Silas. He's my father. I'm his property."

"Then you need to become someone else's property."

She scoffed an acerbic chuckle. "Is it so wrong to want to be no one's property?"

He shook his head. It wasn't wrong. But they had little choice in the matter. It was what it was.

He met her red-rimmed eyes. "So we marry."

"No. We cannot."

"Of course we can." He knew that would be her answer, as it had been countless times before. But now, with her father coming back, he wasn't going to let it go so easily—he wasn't going to let it go at all.

"No." Her head started to swing back and forth. "Hector would never allow it."

"Hector doesn't get a say in the matter. We take time to travel to Scotland. Elope. Then we come back to the Guardians and continue on with our posts. Hector will accept it."

"Or he'll take the title away from you."

"It's already a done deal. Hector wouldn't have told me until it was definite."

She expelled a long sigh. "You know I cannot marry you, Silas."

"There is no reason why you cannot. No *good* reason." Her look pinned him, slicing his heart in two.

He glared back at her—at her stubbornness and her ridiculous resistance. "Those reasons that you think you have—they don't matter."

"Except they do. You will come to resent me."

"Never. You're my best friend, my love. I would never resent you." He dropped down to balance on his heels and set his hands on top of her knees. Her legs jerked, but for once, didn't dodge his touch. "We can and we will do this. Hector doesn't want me on any more jobs until the title he has for me is secure. You can feign an illness for a few weeks. That will give us enough time to get to Scotland and back. And with the title—that title is what we have always needed. Power comes with it and it will afford us more security than we ever could have dreamed of." His fingers squeezed, desperate, into the fabric of her dark violet dress draped over her legs. "Tell me we can do this. I cannot lose you, Josie. I refuse it."

Uncertainty reigned on her delicate features for long breaths, until finally, surrender. She nodded. "Fine. I'll marry you."

{ CHAPTER 1 }

It had to be done. There wasn't anything for it.

It *had* to be done.

Georgina pulled the dark shawl around her shoulders and slipped through the cool night air into the gardens that sat behind the London townhouse her uncle had rented for the season. A season where she was supposed to, finally, find a grand love match.

Her aunt and uncle had put off bringing them to the London marriage mart long enough—so this was to be the year both she and her sister, Willow, were expected to find matches.

They certainly had the inheritances to make the grand matches happen. Love or not.

That had been their very first folly upon entering the marriage mart. Too-large dowries, ripe for the taking, always dredged up the worst muck of the *ton*. They should have realized that when they arrived in London.

Her second folly—one that was hers and her alone— she was about to meet head-on.

Passing by the wrought-iron metal gate, she turned and let the cool metal slip from her fingers as she closed the gate without a sound. She'd been in a stupor for the last two days, trying to reconcile the news in her mind, all to no avail. So she needed action.

Action. A plan would help her. Would pull her out of the shock.

Her feet quick across the coaching lane to the shadows along the mews, she slipped into the carriage house and headed directly to the sleek black coach with her family's crest on the side. The robin and the rose entwined above a ship were barely visible in the light of the one lit lantern that hung along the wall in the front of the building. The crest that had been her father's, once upon a time, before he died and left her and Willow in the care of their uncle and aunt.

The carriage door opened in front of her. She quickly found her footing on the step that had been pulled and lifted herself up into the confines of the carriage, closing the door behind her as she sat on the back cushions.

His scent enveloped her, a scent she had once found earthy and exciting and dangerous. Hay and horse touched with an indescribable scent that unconsciously made her tongue water.

Leroy's hands were instantly on her upper arms, pulling her into him. "I got yer note." He leaned in, trying to find her lips with his.

Georgina threw her hand up, pressing against his chest to stop him, and she pulled back as much as his grip on her would allow. "Obviously."

Leroy was a simple man, a coachman was all he would ever be, but he would have to do. She didn't have much choice.

She pushed at his chest harder, scooting her backside into the corner of the bench, as far as she could away from him. "And no, Leroy. This isn't about that."

She'd stopped meeting him for these misguided trysts a month ago, yet he had refused to give up on what they had shared, convinced she would fall back into his arms. She had another opinion. She had no intention of repeating her transgressions with him. Ever.

At her coldness, he stiffened and his fingers tightened, digging into her upper arms before he forcibly relaxed himself and released her. "Then what is it about?"

There was no use prolonging what she most wanted to avoid.

"I'm with child."

He jumped back on the bench like she had just grown two extra heads. "What?"

"Do you really need me to repeat it?"

It took him a long moment, his look going everywhere in the carriage but at her, before he shook his head. "How long?"

She shifted, rearranging the shawl around her shoulders that he'd set askew when he'd grabbed her. Her arms folded under her now-heavy breasts. "I don't know, a month, maybe more."

"How do ye not know?"

Her glare whipped up to him. "I don't know how these matters work. I haven't exactly been able to ask any trusted source about it. I just found out for certain two days past."

In truth, it was Georgina's modiste that had mentioned that her body had changed, then discreetly gave her the

name of a midwife in the East End she could visit to find out the reality of the situation.

"Yer right. I'm sorry." His head was still shaking, and now his hands as well. He clasped the thick, strong fingers tight together to still them. Fingers she had once reveled in touching her. "Why didn't ye tell me right away?"

"I have been trying to. Trying to get you alone, but it has been difficult."

His eyes narrowed at her. "Because Miss Sanders keeps getting in the way. She has been for a long time, now." A malicious glint flickered in his eyes that sent a shiver down her spine.

Surely she misread it. Aside from her uncle, Leroy was the kindest man she'd ever met.

"Miss Sanders is only doing her job—she's keeping Lord Fugal and his disgusting cousins away from me and Willow, which has become quite a chore for her."

"I told you I would protect you from those wastrels."

"Except you cannot. You cannot be inside the balls and the dinners. Miss Sanders has been invaluable in not only protecting me, but Willow as well."

"Yes, but she's been keeping every other man with a beating pulse away from ye as well. Including me."

Her shoulders lifted. "I agree, that is unfortunate as I have needed to speak with you."

"And she hasn't allowed it. Not for a bloody month."

This wasn't what she came here for—she had far more pressing matters than Leroy's growing ire at his lack of access to her. But it was clear she needed to placate him before they could move onto the real conversation they needed to have.

She reached out, setting her fingers on his forearm. "I do wish I had more freedom from Miss Sanders's watchful eye. But she has become my friend and she is doing exactly what we hired her to do—keep Willow and me safe from untoward advances or from being trapped into marriage by a compromising situation—so I cannot fault her for being excellent at her job."

He nodded, his hands clenching into fists. "But if ye fired her, it would solve the problem."

"Solve the problem?" She waved her hand in the air. "Miss Sanders isn't the problem, Leroy. The problem is that I am with child."

"But is it mine?"

Shock rolled through her body, stilling her tongue and making the world spin around her for several long seconds.

She stared at his handsome face in the shadows, wondering what she ever saw in it.

Of course, that was probably the answer. He was handsome. He doted on her, pined after her. Told her all the things that she had yearned to hear her entire life. All the things that had made her feel valued and loved, at least for a while.

But as for his character? His personality? She'd started to have reservations about those things a month ago and that was when she had broken things off with him.

Except everything had changed—she couldn't afford to judge his character now. Not in her current situation. A babe was growing inside of her. A babe she wanted.

It had crossed her mind to finally let one of those fops of the *ton* into her good graces and to quickly marry him. But she couldn't do it.

No one deserved to be made a cuckold. It was cruel and she would end up living a life of lies.

She set her stare on Leroy. "It is yours. You are the only possibility."

He exhaled a long sigh.

Silent. His stare locked into the upper corner of the carriage like he was considering how he could escape the coach at this moment.

She heaved a sigh. If he wasn't going to say it, she would prompt him until he did. "So what do we do?"

He glanced at her, the right side of his mouth pulling back. "We wait."

"Wait for what?"

"Wait to see if it resolves itself."

Stunned, her body fell backward, her shoulder blades hitting the sidewall of the carriage. "What?"

"Don't look at me that way." Leroy grabbed her hand, pulling her into his chest, trying to comfort her even as her body stiffened at his touch. Heaven help her, she wanted that—comfort. She had been flailing about, trying to not worry herself to death in the past days. That was all she had wanted when she had come out here to meet him. Comfort and a plan.

That neither had emphatically shown up was disconcerting.

His hand went to the back of her head, pushing it onto his chest. "All I am saying, Georgina, is that these things often do…resolve themselves. Or there are methods to help resolve them. Some tonics. A fall. So we should wait."

Methods?

Tonics? Falls?

She twisted her body out of his grip, her voice squeaking. "You want me to lose the babe?"

"I am merely saying we should extend caution. That we do not make hasty plans."

It took her a full breath deep into her lungs before she could compose herself. Straighten her spine.

She looked him straight in the eye, condemning every stupid decision she had made in the last four months in London. "Fine."

{ CHAPTER 2 }

He was obsessed.

There was no other word for it.

Silas was obsessed with Miss Georgina Constantine, which was why he was currently lurking about the woods surrounding Toften Hall at Lady Toften's house party.

He was there to protect her, of course. He took his job as a guardian seriously, though the obsession part of his current assignment would be frowned upon by Hector, head of the Guardian of the Bones.

Not that Hector knew exactly where Silas was these days.

A good thing, for Silas had slipped into unhealthy obsession territory ever since he'd wandered into the hallway at Almack's where Georgina was dressing down Lord Flewman for cutting her sister on the dance floor.

Silas had stood in the shadows around the corner, Georgina's voice sinking into his pores until he was flush with her. He'd only followed her out of the ballroom to ensure that she was safe, as he'd been doing for a month without her knowledge.

Josie's last job, now his to complete.

"What do you think you truly accomplished out there, you abominable dolt?" Georgina's voice had bit through the air, and it had been enough to make Silas freeze and then

sink back behind the corner of the corridor to eavesdrop from under a staircase.

"Dolt?" The outraged puffery in Lord Flewman's voice was comical. "Don't you dare call me—"

"I'll call you anything I want, you miserable heap of walking rubbish. You think you showed all of the *ton* what a *man* you are? Cutting the one person in the room that had even bothered to glance at you?" She had dragged out the word "man" to make sure Lord Flewman knew exactly how small a man she thought he was.

"You think that Willow danced with you because she needed to? You think she would actually throw any favor your way?" Her slippered feet shuffled along the floorboards and Silas envisioned her crowding in on the idiot. "Willow saw instantly what I saw. A pathetic, money-grubbing, snarky troll of a man—and I use the term 'man' lightly—that couldn't find a single female to corner into conversation tonight because you are a supercilious, conceited fop. She danced with you because she is far too prone to pity. And I saw her stifling her breath, trying not to breathe in your rancid breath the entire time you danced. So now I will make it my personal goal to sink any match you think to make this season, you arse."

"You—you cannot—you don't have that power." At the snarl in Lord Flewman's voice, Silas had almost surged forward to intervene, but Georgina's next words stopped him.

"But I do have the money. And that equates to power. That alone will scare off any ladies you think to woo. No one will dare be on my bad side, for the match I make with my inheritance will put me in the highest of circles. Ones that will squash you without a thought, like an ant on a picnic blanket. You can have my pity or you can have my wrath."

"You are a witch, pure and through, Miss Constantine."

"Better a witch than a fool letting the likes of you near my sister. Much less letting you cut her at Almack's." She'd cleared her throat. "Make right what you just did out on that dance floor, Lord Flewman. Tonight. Apologize profusely to her so everyone can hear that you were sick and had to leave the floor mid-dance. It's your only chance."

"And if I don't?"

"Then know I have a long memory. I don't forget. I don't forgive."

Silas had smirked to himself.

Little dragon.

"Fine. But this better be the end of it." Lord Flewman stomped around the corner and back toward the ballroom.

Silas had silently shifted farther back into the shadows of the staircase as Lord Flewman passed him without seeing his presence.

A moment later, Georgina had come around the corner, a determined look still set hard upon her face. Like she had solved the problem but it still vexed her to no end.

Which it probably did.

He didn't imagine this was the first conversation of that particular ilk that she'd had in darkened hallways with fools that had chosen to carelessly handle their interactions with her sister, Willow. Willow was just as beautiful as Georgina, had the exact same inheritance, but she had an oddity that had marked her as undesirable within the circles of the *ton*.

Georgina had probably been delivering dress-downs just like that her entire life. She was an older sister, and older sisters tended to be protective.

And just like that, Silas had become obsessed with Georgina.

Obsessed with her voice. Obsessed with who she was dancing or talking with. Obsessed with the scent of her—tropical mangoes and pineapples twisted with cinnamon that trailed after her. Obsessed with the dragon heart that beat with fire in her blue eyes. Light blue eyes that were haunting and piercing at the same time. Eyes that took stock of everything around her.

An obsession, full and through, before he'd even been introduced to her.

He'd made sure to traverse that particular barrier his first night at Lady Toften's house party in Buckinghamshire. Then he'd made sure to make the space next to Georgina, *his* space. Not obvious. Not overbearing as so many of these suitors. A dance here and there. Partners at whist. Falling in step with her on the way to one of the many activities Lady Toften had planned for the house party.

Just enough attention to make her seek him out whenever she entered a room.

The first time she had pointedly done so was when she'd entered the library two nights past. He always knew when she entered a room—could sense her presence in his bones. And when her look had skittered across the room until it landed on him and stuck, the elation he'd felt in his chest was near to unbearable. He'd almost jumped up and crushed her into the wall with his body and his lips.

He'd stayed in place on the settee, of course. With his leg crossed casually over his knee and not the slightest hiccup in his conversation with Lord Gruston.

He couldn't very well show the world that his thoughts were solely on the woman paused at the library doorway.

But the thought was there, rampant in his head. Of Georgina's body pressed up against his. Of her soft gasps as his hands travelled over her body. Of her tongue tangling with his. Of her thighs clasped tight around his waist.

That space next to her was now his—at least for the moment—and dammit to all hell, he wanted her.

Something he hadn't expected when he'd first set out to finish Josie's mission—to protect the Constantine sisters.

Diving into an obsession with the person you were protecting was definitely frowned upon. Guardians guarded—they didn't obsess.

This had never happened to him before and it was unhealthy. Needing to be near Georgina. Needing her scent in his nose. Needing her words echoing in his ears.

Hence his current lurking about the woods surrounding Toften Hall.

He knew the ladies had planned to go swimming at the waterfall on Toften grounds while the men had gone hunting, and he had slipped away from the party soon after the hunt started.

He needed to make sure the sisters were fine and not in danger.

Or so he told himself.

Ten minutes ago, he'd watched the group of ladies laughing as they stumbled along through the woods on their way back to the main hall, their shifts and dresses soaked through after spending the afternoon at the waterfall.

Willow hadn't been in the party, so he'd been waiting for her to appear on the trail, debating on whether to go to the waterfall to make certain the younger Constantine sister was fine and had chosen to stay at the pool. Even with that worry on his mind, he couldn't shake the image of Georgina laughing, dropping her boots as she had walked by with the other ladies. The curve of her backside against the wet cloth as she bent over to pick up the boots. Her blond-red hair wet and dangling about her shoulders. The smile on her face that he felt oddly jealous of.

He wanted to put the smile there. *He* wanted to own it—the happiness.

As though his thoughts alone could manifest her out of thin air, Georgina suddenly reappeared on the trail that led back to the waterfall.

Having her this close. Wet. Disheveled.

It was too much for him.

He stepped out of the cover of the trees where he had been hiding, a seemingly innocent look on his face as he saw her.

She jumped at the crunch of his footfalls over some twigs, spinning toward him as she held her boots and the shift she hadn't bothered to put on under her dress against her ribcage. Panic turned into delight as her eyes lit up at the sight of him. "Lord Atwell—Silas—you scared me. I thought all of the men had gone on the hunt."

"They did. But killing is not on the top of my list, so I dropped off from the party as soon as it was reasonable."

Her brow furrowed. "Was Lord Fugal on the hunt with his cousins?"

Why in the hell was she asking about Lord Fugal? A shard of jealousy shot through his gut.

Jealousy?

He was never jealous. There was no need for the emotion. But there it was, plain as day, eating away at his innards.

He set an easy smile on his face. "He was. He and his cousins were at the front of the pack, bloodthirsty."

Her nose wrinkled. "I would expect no less of the man."

The way she said the words perked his attention. He knew Josie had been protecting the sisters from overzealous suitors, but this—the tone in her voice as she mentioned Lord Fugal—was something more.

His eyebrows lifted to her. "Has Lord Fugal slighted you in some way?"

She waved her free hand. "It is nothing. I am only concerned on my sister. I left her at the waterfall as she wanted to swim, but not with the other ladies, so I ushered the rest of them back to the hall so she could have privacy. She does like to swim, but I wasn't about to leave her alone in the woods."

"With Lord Fugal lurking about?"

She looked up at him sharply. "With anyone lurking about. I presume I don't need to tell you about our ridiculous dowries."

He shook his head. He'd heard about little else since he'd arrived at Toften Hall.

How Georgina was the catch of the season with her beauty, poise and vast amount of money attached to her. Which bachelor was the most likely to catch her. His own name bandied about by the gossips.

He inclined his head toward her. "I will admit I have seen that the dowry has brought some of the most conniving scraps of the *ton* to your doorstep."

"Maddeningly so." She sighed. "It has caused us more trouble than it would ever be worth. I wish I could have convinced my uncle to change his mind on the amount, but it was not to be."

"Does he regret it now?"

Her shoulders lifted, the slight line of her collarbone pushing against the damp light peach fabric of her dress. "I don't know that he would admit to it. But he must see it. Though I do not fault him for what he's done—it is our inheritance and he just wants to see us happy, but I don't know that he realizes all the trouble that it has set afoot."

"Trouble?" The hairs on the back of his neck spiked.

"It is nothing, truly. Forget I said anything on the matter." She forced a too-wide smile. "Willow and I are very fortunate to have been doted upon by my aunt and uncle. We are grateful for the enviable position that we are in."

"Yet it isn't enviable, is it?"

She paused, a frown settling on her face as she studied him. "No, not truly. It has made me very distrustful of anyone that talks to me."

"Including me?"

She nodded. "Including you."

Silas was surprised by her honesty, yet found it refreshing. Georgina was not one to play coy games. Something to admire.

"You don't look taken aback." The frown on her face lessened. "Most men don't care for that about me."

"Honesty?"

She nodded.

"I do." He leaned slightly toward her, his voice low. "I care for it a great deal."

Her cheeks flushed and he was having a devil of a time keeping his fingers from reaching out to feel the heat chasing up her neck.

She gave a little shake of her head, a breathless chuckle coming from her throat. The soft sound of it so unique to her and so vulnerable it cut straight into his chest.

"I don't know what to say to you, Silas. I don't know how to banter. How to be coy."

"That is the last thing I want from you. Banter. Coyness."

"What is it that you do want?"

What did he want? He wanted every one of her breaths, every inch of her body, all of her words.

Yet he would be a fool to admit it at this juncture. While he'd been shadowing her for a month, she had only known him for a week.

"What I want?" He bit his words back, his look dropping down her body and for the life of him, he couldn't take his eyes off of her rosy nipples that were clearly visible through the damp cloth of her dress, the mere sight of them sending his cock to full attention.

Though he attempted to temper his voice, his words came out in a husky growl, leaving it hard to mistake the heat running through his blood and making him itch to touch her. "The things I want from you are not speakable. So don't ask for them, little dragon."

{ CHAPTER 3 }

Silas's look had dropped down her body, and on instinct, Georgina glanced down at herself.

Her dress had soaked through, her erect nipples visible through the light peach muslin.

She froze, the heat crawling up her neck searing her. Mortified she had been walking through the woods with her nipples on display for anyone to see.

But if anyone was to see them, she wasn't exactly saddened that it was Silas with his stare locked on them. She had been thinking about this man too much since meeting him last week. So much so that when they had shifted to given names, she hadn't thought twice about the intimacy. It had just seemed right.

But she was thinking about him when she had no right to entertain any thoughts at all about him. Not with the reality of what was happening to her at the moment.

Don't go there, fool. Nothing can ever—ever—happen with him.

She groaned inwardly at the vicious little voice in her head. The one that loved to tell her at every chance that she was idiot.

She heaved an inward sigh, ignoring the voice, as she needed to get back to the moment at hand.

Her options at this juncture with Silas were very limited.

Pretend outrage that he dared to be looking at her body. Or pretend nothing was amiss.

Neither was a great choice.

Her only saving grace in this matter was that her shift was draped over her arm and hid the crux of her thighs from his eyes. That would be the ultimate embarrassment— the dark of her curls showing through the fabric. She clutched her boots and the shift tighter to her ribcage.

Then again, there was a third choice at this juncture. She always did like a third choice.

There was nothing to do but take this head-on.

She lifted her look to Silas. His stare intent on her nipples, the dark heat in the hazel streaks of his eyes almost took her aback. The tip of his tongue darted out and he slowly licked his lips. Lips that weren't too thick or thin— perfectly proportioned just like the rest of the strong lines of his face. The drag of his tongue across his lips was the most fascinatingly sinful thing she'd ever witnessed, burning an instant need deep in her core.

Stop.

Stop any and all those thoughts.

He was out of reach. He always would be.

It took her a full breath to compose herself enough for words. She kept her arm holding her shift and boots in place, stubbornly refusing to move them upward to cover her breasts from his view. "It appears as though my nipples are out in the world for all to see. I apologize if they offend you."

His gaze jerked up to her face. "There is not a single thing about you that offends me, Georgina."

Well…hell.

She didn't think it possible, but the man just grew tenfold in her esteem. Not to mention setting her mouth to water.

Her look sank to his lips. Those glorious lips with just the perfect amount of pink to them. The air between them thickened until it was near to choking, and still she was stuck in place, unable to move away or conjure any more words.

She didn't need any more.

For he took a decisive step forward and leaned down, sliding his arm around her waist as his delicious lips landed on hers. A kiss that took a hold of her at once, heated and raw and she could feel the pounding lust throbbing along his throat under her fingers she hadn't realized she had lifted to wrap around his neck.

The vein against his throat pounded in a frenzied beat as the back of his neck tensed, his muscles bridling what he really wanted to do to her. Which she could only surmise was to lift her against the nearest tree and slam his shaft into her.

That he was holding hard against the torture in his body took her breath away, leaving her only wanting more. More of the kiss. More of him.

His tongue delved deep, exploring, and the taste of him invaded her tongue. More. She wanted more of him. Of his taste. Of his smell. Of this kiss that curled her toes.

Drowning. She was drowning in everything about him, as though they were encased in a bubble holding only the two of them, breathing each other's air, drowning together.

She couldn't afford to drown.

Not now.

Not ever.

Her hand dropped from his neck and she set it onto his chest between them and pushed, breaking the kiss.

The second their lips parted, her hand flew up, her fingertips on her lips which heated and pulsated with every heartbeat. "I am sorry—I cannot let this go any further. While I like you—tremendously so—I cannot let it continue."

"Georgina—"

"No." She hiked her arm holding her shift and boots higher on her body, hiding her breasts. "No, I have to find Willow. Please forgive me for kissing you. I never should have…"

She cut off her own words as she turned away from him, her steps moving fast down the trail. Even with that, she glanced back at him only to see him adjusting himself, and the sight of it sent a wicked pang through her core.

Admirable that he didn't insist she stay. Didn't try to take it further.

He had control where she didn't.

She never should have let herself think for one second that there could be any future for her other than what was already in store.

Her life was now on a very specific path of her own making.

It didn't matter what she thought of Silas, or how her body ached for him, or how her heart started to quicken every time he would stroll over to her and start a conversation. It didn't matter that his words were the only thing that had buoyed her spirit during the last week at this house party.

None of that mattered and it wouldn't do any good to dream otherwise.

Not even for a stolen minute in the woods.

{ CHAPTER 4 }

"Did she die fast?"

Silas slammed the coachman— Leroy Wilkins—into the inside wall of the stable, the edge of his blade digging into the vulnerable flesh across the man's neck.

The coachman's body froze, but his eyes were frantic, looking for escape. Except there was no escape, no intervention by a stable hand or another driver stepping into the barn. Silas had made sure of it. Made sure they were alone.

Realizing there was no escape, a manic laugh shook up from the coachman's chest.

Silas grabbed the front of his coat, dragging him forward and then slamming him against the wall again. Dust and debris from the open boards rained down from the impact and all the air rushed out of Mr. Wilkins's chest, coughs spurting out uncontrolled. His neck flexed against Silas's blade and blood started to seep onto the silver.

His patience near to snapping, Silas shoved his nose close to the face of the dung heap of a man, his voice a growl. "I asked you a question. Did she die fast?"

"I don't know what yer talking about and I'm not telling ye a thing, nob."

It had taken a month to find a witness to Josie's murder. To find someone that reported Josie didn't trip and fall, didn't carelessly step out onto that street. She never would have. She always knew her surroundings. And the last thing she was, was clumsy.

It had taken too long, but Silas had found the boy—a chimney sweep that had been directly behind the costermonger that had been within five feet of the carriage trampling Josie. The costermonger hadn't witnessed what had happened. But the boy had seen it. Seen it in whole. Described perfectly what Josie had been wearing that day, down to her shoes. The boy had witnessed everything, and that boy had just yesterday identified Mr. Wilkins—Georgina's family coachman—as the one that had pushed Josie into the path of that coach.

And now the bastard thought to play stupid.

Silas pressed the blade deeper into the cut on the man's throat. "Except you will tell me or I will carve you up like the pig you are. I already know you were there that day Miss Sanders died, and I know you did it, so now you're going to answer the damn question unless you want torture to be part of the day." He slammed him one more time into the wall. "Did she die fast?"

Mr. Wilkins stilled, his gaze suddenly defeated as impending death flashed in front of his eyes. He stayed silent for a long moment, refusing to look at Silas seething in his face, before the wretched evil inside of him etched onto his too-pretty face.

Mr. Wilkins smirked, a snicker vibrating his chest.

Growling, Silas slammed him into the rough boards again, stealing his breath. "You were there—did she die fast?"

A sneer curved across the bastard's lips, his face turning ugly. "No, the bitch died slow, painful. I could see it in her eyes—the wretched torture of her bones being crushed by those horses and that coach, lying there in the dung of the street, knowing death was coming for her but not quick enough. She lasted longer than I thought she would. Fighting it, moaning. The bitch got exactly what was coming to her. An end ripe with torture and disbelief."

Bright red filled Silas's eyes and all he could think of was to destroy—destroy everything around him, including this monster.

But he had one last question for the man.

The one thing in all of this that didn't make sense.

Silas blinked. Blinked again and again until he could see Mr. Wilkins's face through the haze of red blinding him. "Why?"

"Why?" Another twisted chuckle spit out of his lips. "That bitch thought she was better than me—she was keeping me away from Georgina. But Georgina didn't want that. She wanted me."

"Georgina wanted you? What in the hell are you talking about?"

"Yer fine lady liked to muck about in the hay with the help, or didn't ye know that about her? I seen how ye look at her. But know she liked the cock on me. Liked it too much."

His words twisted in Silas's head—flailed about, like frantic bees in a jar, not making any sense.

He shook his head. "You're lying."

"Am I? Or does yer fine lady love my cock so much that she was the one that told me to get rid of Miss Sanders? Begged me to do it. Sanders was keeping us apart and Georgina didn't want to be apart. Not anymore. Ye want to kill someone for it, go into the fancy hall and slice the throat of that witch. Slice the throat of one of yer own."

Georgina?

No. Absolutely not.

Not Georgina. Never.

Shock rolled through Silas, sending a tremble through his limbs.

Georgina could no sooner order the murder of Josie than kill a fly on her arm.

Mr. Wilkins's eyes squinted at him. "What? No clue one of yer own could be just as heartless as the worst of us? Just as evil?" Mr. Wilkins started cackling. "Such an idiot. And I was just her little puppet, I did it all for her and I didn't ev—"

His blade sliced clean across Mr. Wilkins's neck, cutting the man's voice, blood sputtering out with puffs of air from his lungs that had been meant for words.

Words he would never speak.

The coachman slumped down slowly, his body heavy against the wall of the stable until he fell forward flat on his face.

Silas kicked him over with his boot and spat on him. A far better death than the man deserved after murdering Josie.

He walked out of the barn, wiping off the blood that had splattered onto his hand on the side of his dark coat.

He needed to clean up—the dark cloth would only hide do so much.

The early morning sunlight hit his face and he squinted, looking up at the enormous hall looming just up the hill from the set of three barns that composed the stables at Toften Hall.

After a quick glance around, he turned to the right and quickened his long strides toward the woods that spread outward behind the stables. Most of the guests would be awakening at the moment, now that daylight had appeared. It wouldn't do to be seen near the stables.

Silas skirted along the edge of the forest, intending to go around the sheep field until he arrived at the main drive up to the hall.

A morning walk to the main road. That's all anyone would think if they spotted him.

His legs moved, knowing their destination even as his mind reeled, all of his thoughts in a whirlwind.

Georgina?

He didn't believe it. Couldn't believe it.

He liked Georgina, genuinely liked her—was bloody well obsessed with her—and not just as part of the role he was playing. He liked the banter as they danced, her quick wit and her fierce defense of anyone looking cross-eyed at her younger sister. He liked the tropical scent of her. He liked most of all how she looked at him with fire brewing just below the surface of her piercing blue eyes.

He damn well liked the woman—had even determined he would start to court her until she pushed him away in the woods after their kiss—and she had been the one that had sent Josie to her death?

No. *Impossible.*

Josie had been protecting Georgina. It's why he had wormed his way into Georgina's life in the first place—to finish what Josie had been unable to do. To protect the Constantine sisters. Josie's last job.

If he hadn't also been using Georgina to investigate Josie's death, he would have wooed her long ago. The unabashed wantonness in her eyes when she looked at him had told him she was far more experienced than her aunt and uncle knew or what society would expect out of a debutante like her.

Hell. He had thought to do that very thing—have her in his bed, if not more. But only after he'd found Josie's murderer.

And Georgina had killed her—killed his wife?

Impossible.

His strides slowed.

But why would Mr. Wilkins have bothered to lie? He was a dead man no matter what and he knew it. Especially after what the man told him of Josie's death. How she died, the pain of it. He was a dead man taking his last breaths.

Those seconds before death? Those were seconds of confessions. They always were.

Bile soured his tongue, darkness twisting deep in his gut. Twisting everything he had felt during the past weeks about that woman into the vile need to make her suffer. Suffer just as Josie did.

Georgina.

He had touched the despicable creature. Laughed with her. *Lusted* after her.

A betrayal to Josie with each breath he'd spent in the witch's presence.

His stride started again. He'd thought he'd feel a sense of relief at Mr. Wilkins's death. But it didn't help. Josie was still gone.

Not that he regretted killing the man.

There wasn't happiness in vengeance, but there was peace. He could taste the cruel promise of it at the tip of his tongue, even if he couldn't quite swallow it yet.

He looked up at the ostentatious hall as he drew closer, looking at the window he knew was Georgina's, and his mouth pulled into a tight line.

Just one more loose end to tie up and Josie's spirit could be at peace. Not haunting him nightly in his sleep as she did.

Just one loose end.

Making Georgina pay for killing his wife.

{ CHAPTER 5 }

Georgina smiled up at Lord Atwell.

It was a shame, truly, for Silas was the first man she had met during the season that she actually liked. The first man that wasn't clearly after her dowry or out for a quick tryst in the back corner of some gardens.

He'd shown uncharacteristic kindness to her sister, Willow, during the last week, and for that alone, she could have very well fallen in love with the man.

It didn't hurt that he was handsome in a way that made her lower belly tighten and her thighs clench together under her skirts for how his laugh made her core tighten.

And that kiss in the woods had set every tiny nerve in her body aflame, making her want so much more with him.

He was very close to being someone she could love, even knowing she couldn't dare walk anywhere near the edge of that treacherous canyon.

As much as she would like to consider a future with Silas—it could never be. All because she had done a grand job of fully mucking up her own life.

It was time to un-muck it up.

No matter how she loathed what she was about to do.

She glanced back over her shoulder to find Willow amongst the large group of guests that had descended on Toften Hall for the house party. Heads were bobbing about, the women in their finest riding garb. Excited chatter filled the air as they made their way to the stables to set out on

the ride two hours to the west to visit the Roman ruins that sat along Lady Toften's brother's land.

The group fanned out and Georgina and Silas stopped in front of the line of horses, all saddled and ready for the ride.

There. Georgina finally spotted Willow next to Lord Fugal at the end of the line.

Not good. That bastard was always trying to corner one of them. Always trying to threaten them.

Just as Georgina was about to excuse herself from Silas to intervene between Lord Fugal and Willow, her sister managed to step away from Lord Fugal after Lady Toften interrupted the two of them. Sitting atop her mare, their hostess waved her hands toward the last of the three barns that had been built as smaller versions of the main house, the facades just as grand. Georgina doubted that even with this large of a party, all of the stables were in use.

She exhaled a sigh of relief as Willow skirted away from the horses. She should have expected it—trusted her sister more. Willow was adept at slipping away from Lord Fugal no matter how hard he tried to corner her to salivate all over her.

Willow could handle herself, but ingrained habits died hard. Georgina had spent a lifetime watching over her little sister and intervening when there was the slightest threat to Willow's happiness. It had left them sheltered, staying mostly at the family's estate in Essex throughout their lives. But Georgina wouldn't have it any other way. Her sister's happiness was worth any sacrifice.

"I hope your dress will keep you warm. Lady Toften insists that the weather will hold today, but I don't think she's correct."

"What?" Georgina's look swung toward Silas next to her, only half-hearing his words, her eyebrows raised. There was too much in her mind at the moment for idle chitchat.

Rude, but after today she would likely never see Silas again. Never see most of these people. Or rather, most of these people would never see her, for she would be an outcast from polite society.

She just prayed her downfall wouldn't rub off on Willow. She rather liked the gentleman, Mr. Thatcher, that had been paying her sister lots of attention during these last weeks. If she guessed correctly, Mr. Thatcher rather liked Willow, even if her sister was too dense to notice it.

Silas inclined his head toward the west. "The clouds seem to be building. I think we'll be caught in a storm by the time we get to the ruins."

She looked at him for just a moment too long without replying, but that happened to her with Silas. He was sinfully handsome, yes, but it was his voice that did it to her. Thick and low and smooth like the tastiest morning chocolate sliding down into her belly.

"As long as we get to the ruins before the rain begins, there are several structures nearby that we can shelter under. I don't know that the horses will be happy about it, but we should stay dry enough." She stretched a smile across her face, feigning interest in the group's destination, even though she knew it wasn't about to be her destination. Her

traveling satchel was already hidden away in the middle stable.

"You've been to the ruins before?" Silas asked.

"I have. Lady Toften and my aunt are close friends from when they were young. We've been to Toften Hall before—though never during a house party like this one. It is usually just me, Willow, my aunt, and Lady Toften when we visit. Though—"

A piercing scream cut her words.

Willow's scream.

Her look instantly scoured the crowd outside the stables lining up for horses. There. Lord Fugal and his two cousins in plain view.

Thank the heavens.

But where was Willow?

Another scream and she saw Lord Fugal start to run toward the last barn.

Georgina followed suit, pushing through the guests in her frantic bid to get to her screaming sister.

She got to the entrance of the barn, her eyes not adjusting to the dim light quick enough.

"Good Lord, sir." Horrified, a stable hand with his hand over his mouth stumbled backward into the people in front of her, blocking her path.

"Willow—Willow—where are you? Willow!" Georgina screamed and she pushed through the crowd that had gathered at the barn's entrance. Three men, two women, and the stable hand and she was through the throng of bodies.

"Georgie, I'm here. I'm fine." Her back to the wall of the barn, Willow emerged from behind Mr. Thatcher, pushing off his hold on her. A hold like he was attacking her or saving her?

Georgina ran at full speed toward Willow and grabbed her shoulders, her frantic gaze sweeping over her sister. No blood, nothing amiss, not even a hair out of place. But Georgina wasn't relieved, not by far. "I heard you scream—what is that?" Her gaze had shifted into the stable next to them. The tip of a head she could see past the low half wall of the stable caught her eye.

The tip of a head on the ground.

She jabbed a step closer.

"Georgie—no." Willow screamed at her, her hand grazing her arm, but Georgina was already out of reach, her stare focused on the tip of the head.

Closer.

The face.

Leroy.

Blood splattered across his cheek. His eyes wide open. Glassy.

His neck.

Sliced open. Blood, thick and dried and crusting along the gaping wound.

Her jaw dropped as she tried to suck air into her throat, but only an odd wheezing sound filled her mouth.

Her hands went up onto her own neck, like she could somehow close up the vicious wound across his throat with her own motions. "N—n—no—no—no." A strangled whisper cut out of her mouth.

Willow jumped in front of her. "Georgie, no, don't look. Don't look at it."

She stumbled a step backward, her arms wrapping around her waist as she spun, shoving her way through the people crowding the entrance of the barn. Murmured whispers filling her ears as she staggered out into daylight.

A horse.

She needed a horse.

There. A sidesaddle on a horse with no one atop.

She ran for it, hiked her foot high into the stirrup and she grabbed the pommel, yanking herself onto the seat.

Heels into the horse's flanks and then all she could hear were the hooves thundering into the ground.

"Georgie!" Willow's scream echoed in her ears, but it seemed lifetimes away. Not enough to turn back to. Not enough to be safe in.

She had been set to elope with Leroy—minutes away from it.

And now he was dead. But his babe still sat deep in her belly.

She rode.

Rode hard and fast. Her body shaking. Tears streaming down her face.

Rode for what seemed like hours.

Rode until the tears started to mix with the sheets of rain falling from the sky, blinding her.

Rode until a low branch hit her directly across her shoulders and the horse flew out from under her.

Air. Air beneath her for a suspended half a second and then the brutal, unforgiving ground crashed into her.

Crushing everything. Shocks of pain vibrating up her body. Stealing away every drop of breath in her lungs.

Everything wrong.

Everything wrong.

Pain sliced across her lower abdomen. Burning agony centered deep within her.

Everything wrong.

{ CHAPTER 6 }

He found her.

Silas blinked, droplets of rain dripping off his eyelashes, the brim of his hat not enough to keep the blinding downpour off his face.

Behind Willow, he had been the second one onto a horse to go after Georgina once he'd realized she had darted to a mare and taken off.

Her lover dead. How sad for her.

Any last remnants of doubt he had about Georgina's innocence washed away in that instant. The cry in her throat had been one of anguish—the anguish of losing a lover.

There had been no mistaking it.

Willow had a slight head start on him. But he was determined to find Georgina first. It had taken hours of traversing these woods, searching, to find her. And now this. He was the first one.

A gift he hadn't seen coming.

Georgina didn't have a clue he was there, in the thick of the woods at an angle back away from her.

With her body slumped against a tree, her hands moved in front of her, though he couldn't tell what she was doing from this angle. Her horse wasn't in sight.

Still a furlong away, he slid off his horse and tied the reins to the nearest branch.

The rain started to ease as he crept along between the trees toward her at an angle from behind. He paused, bending over, and his fingers wrapped around a hefty stone half buried in moss. Wedging it back and forth, he silently pulled the stone free from the ground and continued forward.

The chill of the wet stone seeped into his palm, and he shifted it in his hand, measuring the weight of it.

Kill her now.

Be done with this whole business.

Be done and set Josie to rest.

If he did it quick he wouldn't have to listen to Georgina's tears and begging and lies. But quick was a mercy she didn't deserve, a mercy not afforded to Josie.

Bile ran across his tongue and any last vestiges of his weak resolve hardened.

Quick. It would have to be quick.

Five steps away. Three. Two.

He lifted the stone high above his head, his stare focusing in on the center of her skull, her jaunty mint green hat long gone, her red-blond hair now matted to her scalp. Impact point.

One.

An anguished cry ripped into the air and her body curled forward.

He held back, his muscles straining against the resistance he forced into his arm.

Agony. A scream of pure anguish pouring out of her body, her soul ripping out of her.

Her torso started to shake furiously and that's when he tore his stare off her skull and looked down at her body.

Blood. So much blood. Her legs bare, jutting up from her bloodied skirt bunched about her waist. The bottom of her white shift soaked in crimson.

He dropped the stone.

Her agony wasn't about some lost lover.

No. Something was grossly wrong with her.

Another wail.

That singular wretched sound twisted something primal deep in his gut.

"Georgina," he said softly, just above a whisper. Though for how her body viciously trembled, he doubted she could hear anything.

He stepped to her side. Closer. "Georgina." This time he said her name louder, loud enough to cut in through any haze in her head.

Her face jerked toward him, even though her eyes were glazed, not seeing anything around her. "Silas?"

He crouched down to rest on his heels, taking in the sweat and tears soaking her face, her hair, her dress.

Her hands moved in front of her, fingers dipping into a lumpy mass of blood between her legs, some of it soaked into the ground. Most of it not.

A babe that was no more.

He set his fingers gently on her shoulder, enough to touch, but not enough to scare her. "Georgina, yes, it's me, Silas."

She gasped back a sob and looked at him, panic setting into her eyes. Panic that was clear even as her body still shook.

"Silas, I don't…I don't know…what I did…I don't know what is…what is happening…what it is doing… what…no…" Her head went down as her hands went into the blood on the forest floor between her legs, digging into the ground, frantically trying to scrape dirt into the mess. "I need to hide it from you…hide it from everyone. You need to go…I need to hide…I need to hide it…I need to…leave, you have to leave." Her words babbled, randomly flipping from incoherent to coherent.

"Georgina, I'm not leaving you in this state."

Her head swung back and forth, fresh tears falling from her cheeks. "No. You cannot know. No one can know."

He slipped his hand across her back to rest along the base of her neck, trying to quell the tremors racking her body. "I already know, Georgina. I know, so I am going to help you."

"You cannot…you need to leave…leave me…leave me to die. I am dying, just like it…I am dying…it's all I deserve…I ruined everything…everything…I don't…you need to leave…"

"I'm not going to do that."

She looked up at him, her blue eyes clear for one moment, piercing him.

And then she swayed, slumping over onto her side, her body scraping downward along the tree.

His breath stilled, and he shifted his fingers along her neck, searching for a pulse. Still strong. She wasn't going to die over this.

He pulled his hand away from her and bowed his head, his hands clasping as he balanced on his heels.

At brutal war with himself for long seconds.

She killed Josie. Killed her.

But he didn't have the heart to dispose of her. Didn't have the heart to put her out of her misery.

And maybe that's what had just been delivered to him.

A misery upon her soul like no other.

But she had to live to suffer it.

So live she would.

{ CHAPTER 7 }

Georgina opened her eyes.

Opened them long enough to recognize that she was in a copper washtub, the warm water enveloping her.

She closed her eyes.

Everything was fuzzy. Shadows and whispers of words around her, though nothing made sense about where she'd been, what had happened since she'd seen Leroy dead in the stables.

Nothing except for one thing.

The thing that was now missing from her belly.

That part, she remembered with brutal clarity.

After that, she couldn't grasp onto any memory securely enough to know what had truly happened.

She heard the murmurs of Willow talking with a maid and then the door clicked closed, silence following.

Heavy silence as her sister walked back to the side of the tub.

It was time to tell Willow the truth.

Not that she could avoid it any longer.

She drew in a trembling breath, her eyes opening as her gaze locked onto the far corner of the tub. "I know you are staring at me."

"Are you in much pain?" Willow sat down on the plush wingback chair next to the bath. An image of Willow sleeping in the chair last night flashed through her mind and a pang of guilt shot across her chest.

"I will survive."

Willow leaned forward, balancing on the edge of the chair, and sighed, her voice ragged. "To be honest, after last night, I'm not sure what to do but look at you. You had me worried and furious. But mostly worried."

"I am sorry." Georgina's stare didn't lift. "Who was that with you last night? I only remember…" Her eyes closed, her head shaking. "Snippets from here and there."

"Do you remember Lord Atwell finding you and bringing you into the cottage?"

She winced. The memory of Silas carrying her into the cottage was one of the few that she knew full well happened. The rest of it—it was as much of a dream as it was reality. "I do. I remember the cottage. And then you were there, pulling my dress off of me. How did you even find me?"

"Lord Atwell. I was with Mr. Thatcher when he found us. We followed him to the cottage."

Her eyes finally lifted, looking to Willow. Even with all that had just happened, worry for her sister was forefront in her mind. "What is Mr. Thatcher to you? I know you have chatted with him many times during the last few days, and he made quite the impression on Lady Toften at Vauxhall. Can he be trusted?"

The edges of Willow's eyes flinched for a mere second, then smoothed out as she schooled her expression. Something her sister wasn't telling her. There had been a lot of that between them during the last months. On both their parts.

Willow nodded. "Yes. He can unequivocally be trusted."

Georgina's brow furrowed. Her sister was usually such a good judge of character, but Mr. Thatcher was a handsome man. Handsome men could turn heads too easily. She knew that first-hand. "How do you know that?"

Willow shrugged. "How do we ever know who to trust and who not to trust? It's the feeling in my bones, and have my bones steered us wrong yet during this season?"

Georgina's lips pursed. "Not yet, but you have only known the man for little more than a fortnight. And you are more akin to label people untrustworthy than to label them trustworthy, so this is suspicious of you."

"That is true, but that more reflects upon the poor composition of society than anything upon myself. I would appreciate it if there were more trustworthy people in our world. Mr. Thatcher is one of those people. I hope Lord Atwell is as well, though I am not sure on the man yet."

The hairs on the back of her neck instantly spiked in defense of Silas. "He can be trusted to not speak of what he saw…I hope." She pulled the washcloth from the water and rubbed it over her face, the weight of everything that had happened yesterday sinking heavy onto her shoulders. Leroy's death. Losing the babe. So much damn pain vibrating through her body that she could barely think. "I want to disappear. I want to sink into the ground and just…vanish."

"That isn't an option, as I still need you on this earth." Willow paused for a long breath and her voice slowed, her words coming carefully. "You were with child, Georgina. How could you not tell me?"

For a long moment Georgina couldn't pull the washcloth from her face. She still needed to hide, if only for a few seconds more.

Realizing her sister was the one person she couldn't hide from, she let the washcloth drop away from her face and met Willow's look directly. "I am sorry. You know everything of me and I know everything of you, yet I couldn't tell you this. I wanted to. So many times."

"What were you thinking to do yesterday? Truly? Not a lie, not a half-truth. What happened? Your reaction to seeing Leroy dead in the stables was extreme—it was a horrific sight, yes—but I thought you had put our coachman from your mind months ago. You told me as much. You weren't supposed to see him anymore—what happened?"

Above the water, Georgina's hand motioned down toward her belly. "This—this happened."

"Why didn't you tell me?"

"Like you are telling me what you are doing with Lord Fugal?" Her look pinned Willow, but then she sighed, her fingers lifting out of the water to run across her brow. "I was with child, Willow. You have to understand that. It was Leroy's child so I had to see him again."

"And what were you thinking to do about the babe?"

"We were going to leave—elope."

Shock dropped Willows jaw, her eyes going wide. "You were going to elope with Leroy?"

"Yes. Yesterday. After the party set out for the Roman ruins, I planned to fall behind and come back to the stables. I already had a satchel packed—it was in the stables with

Leroy. But then it all went so wrong. You screamed and I saw him"—a sob bubbled up from her throat—"I saw all the blood, what my future was, gone, just like that. So I ran. I didn't know what I was doing, other than running. Running from everything. And then this happened. I fell off the horse and then the cramping started, the pain, and I don't remember much of anything after that."

"But why did you run?"

A muffled groan vibrated from Georgina's chest. "It was the only thing to do. I was with child, suddenly with no father. The world just...collapsed around me, so I ran."

"No, the thing to do was to come to me, to tell me of this. Not elope. Not ruin your future." Willow paused, swallowing hard as her look pinned Georgina. "Or...or did you love Leroy and you have been hiding it from me just as you hid the babe you carried?"

"No." Her response was immediate, the word barking from her mouth. Leroy was going to be something she endured. A far thing from love. But she had hoped to eventually settle into an amicable relationship with him. "No, I didn't love him. I know that now, that I never really did. I was just...smitten. He was kind and funny and attentive and handsome and I was a fool. He did have honor, though. He was going to marry me."

And take my fortune. She knew it, but she wouldn't utter it out loud. That lie of omission had been a necessary thing to tell herself in order to secure her future as she needed to.

Willow's mouth twisted to the side. "You were not a fool. And I would have helped you whether you loved him or not. We would have come up with a solution."

"Except there was no solution for this." She looked to Willow, the instinct to protect her little sister beating hard in her chest. "I was trying to keep all of this from you so it wouldn't touch you. The scandal of it all. You have already done too much for me to try and get me out of my transgressions with Leroy in the first place—and look how that turned out. What happened to Miss Sanders. I couldn't put more onto you. I couldn't risk your safety as well."

It was true. Lord Fugal and his cousins had threatened her and Willow with everything under the sun after they had witnessed Georgina and Leroy together, naked, in one of the family's coaches. Back when she was in the whirlwind of the grandness and possibility of London and the attention that Leroy showered onto her. She had fallen for every bit of the charm he had worked her with, when she should have had her head on straight from the moment they stepped foot into London.

All of it, a mess from the start. A mess that had only gotten more complicated once Lord Fugal determined he would blackmail her or Willow into marrying him. Not that the odious man cared for either of them—he merely wanted their fortunes and hadn't hidden that fact for a second.

"Except you can—you can always tell me anything." Willow exhaled a long breath. "And I told you I was taking care of Fugal and his cousins."

"Yes. You said you were taking care of Fugal, but now Leroy is dead. What does that tell you? I never should have

let you talk me into this. Blind trust. Ridiculous." Her
hand splashed in the water. She'd been so utterly stupid and
wrapped up in her own problems—so worried after she'd
found out she was with child—that she'd let Willow take
on the burden of their defense against Lord Fugal. Just one
more mistake to add to the ever-growing list. "The bastards
must have known that I planned on eloping, as Fugal and
his cousins have not left me alone."

"Wait. What?" Alarm seeped into Willow's blue eyes, a
match to her own. "They haven't? What have they done?"

Georgina's shoulders lifted out of the water. "They are
just there, around every turn. At every ball. Every party. In
every room ever since we arrived at Toften Hall. They are
always there, so what am I to think?"

Willow's hands curled into fists. "I am handling them."

She didn't like the fire lighting in her sister's eyes.
Determination. And determination with her sister usually
meant trouble. "You told me that, but how? You haven't
told me anything about what you are planning, just to trust
you to handle it. You have kept just as many secrets from
me, as I from you, Willow."

Her sister stood from the chair and moved to the edge
of the tub, looking down at her. "Just trust me, Georgie,
you have to do that. I am handling them." She bent down
to kiss her forehead. "This will all be over soon and we can
go back to the business of finding you a splendid match.
Just finish bathing and then rest for the day. I will make the
appropriate excuses below, say that you are not feeling well."

Willow was placating her, not telling her anything.
That alarmed her more than anything.

She wanted to reach out and grab her sister's hand and stop her from whatever she was planning.

She wanted to tell Willow that she had failed her. That she'd been so consumed by her own predicament that she'd been a walking shadow, unable to see the world around her and what was happening to her sister.

She wanted to confess all of it, but sometimes, the truth was the hardest thing to admit to those one loved the most.

Instead, she swallowed down all the things she wanted to say and flipped her hand in the air, then caught Willow's fingers. "You cannot keep this from me, Willow, whatever you are planning. I need to protect you and you have that glint in your eye that tells me you are not thinking straight."

"I am thinking straighter than I ever have in my life, Georgie." Willow's lips pursed. "Believe me when I say I know exactly how to handle Fugal and his cousins."

Georgina stared up at her, worry swallowing her whole. But she was in no position to stop her sister. Her body, her mind, and her nerves were all in tatters at the moment. Her capacity for anything beyond the pain surging though her heart and blood had become nonexistent.

She let go of Willow's hand.

Sleep.

She needed sleep. Sleep and then she would tackle her sister once more. Tackle going on about life as though nothing had happened.

Sleep.

Without another word, Willow left the room.

Lord Fugal was too awful, and he was going to ruin her sister, she could feel it in her bones.

But she was in no position to stop it.

Not today.

{ CHAPTER 8 }

"You have to help me."

Just as Silas stepped out of the library at Toften Hall, Georgina jumped out of the shadows and grabbed his hand, pulling him through the hallways toward the orangery that was empty at this time of the evening.

He hadn't talked to Georgina alone since the day he'd found her bloody in the woods. In the days since then, they'd had light, inconsequential conversations here and there amongst larger groups of people. They'd sat side by side on the hillside at the outing to the neighboring estate to gaze at stars. Placed next to each other at dinners. Partners in lawn tennis, and then battledore and shuttlecock.

Every one of those times they'd always been surrounded by other people. Their words to each other stilted and awkward, both of them had been attempting to put on an easygoing façade for onlookers. False smiles. False laughter. False words.

Everything about Georgina, false.

Everything about him, now equally false.

He had let these last days slip by, dwelling on how exactly he was going to make her pay for Josie's death.

True to form, the first thing the blasted woman— selfish to her core—would say to him when they were finally alone was a demand for help.

He allowed himself to be pulled into the shadows of the tropical trees lining the sides of the orangery. Above

them, stars twinkled and shards of moonlight cut through the glass roof. A romantic spot, if one was looking for that.

He was not.

Nor was Georgina, by the look on her face. The sconce in the hallway leading into the glass structure gave dappled light to the panicked look in Georgina's eyes.

He would allow this—letting her go on about whatever her latest crisis was. Maybe another old lover come back to haunt her.

Those days without real interaction with her had given Silas time to think, time to re-steel himself against her.

He'd shown her kindness in the woods when she didn't deserve it, and that was about to change once he decided on his course of action for making her pay for killing Josie.

Until then, he would squash the urge to wrap his hands around her throat and squeeze, and would instead smile at her, listen to her, play the part of an interested suitor.

All the better to eventually sink her.

He contorted his features into sudden concern. "What has happened? Why do you need my help?"

"Willow is gone."

His head snapped back. "Willow is gone? Gone to where?" Regardless of what he thought of Georgina, he rather liked Georgina's younger sister and had been watching with interest the blooming courtship between her and Mr. Thatcher, Jack, during the Toften house party.

She gnawed on her bottom lip. "I don't know. That is the problem. I think Lord Fugal and his cousins may have taken her."

"Lord Fugal took her? Why do you think that?" He
had seen Lord Fugal be a nuisance to both sisters, but the
man was a milksop.

"Because he and his cousins have been threatening both
Willow and myself for months now."

His brows lifted. "They have been threatening you
two?"

She nodded, her hands wringing. "They have been after
our dowries—the money attached to us is too much—too
much—and I told our uncle that after all the snakes started
coming out—that he needed to lower the amount—I told
him. And Lord Fugal has been threatening the most awful
things. Willow said she was handling it, and I let her when
I shouldn't have because I was worried about my own..."
Cutting herself off, she shook her head. "My mind was
elsewhere and I didn't ask enough questions of Willow
about her plans and now she is missing. I fear they took her.
She is gone. They are gone. And I cannot lose her."

"Who else knows of this?"

"Just my aunt and uncle. We are keeping it quiet in
case we have just misplaced her for a moment. You know
she would be completely ruined if she were found in a
compromising position. And I fear the worst."

He stifled a sigh. He too, had been so consumed by
protecting Georgina, that he'd been slack on protecting
Willow as well. Josie would be shaking her head at him
right now if she were alive to see it.

This crisis, he did care about.

He nodded. "How can I help?"

"Mr. Thatcher—he left for London two days ago. He was supposed to return by now. I think he may be able to find Willow, and unless I am incredibly wrong about what I've seen, I believe he has vested interest in doing so. Can you find him? He runs the Alabaster in London. Do you know it?"

"I know it. I can ride tonight."

Relief exploded in her eyes and she set her hand onto his chest, almost slumping into him, though she held herself back from full contact. "Thank you. Thank you so much. You don't know how much this means to me. You've been so kind and I don't know how I can thank you enough."

"No thanks are necessary." He smiled, even though her touch was near to scalding him. Instead of jerking away, he held steady, meeting her look as he slipped his fingers under her chin. "Chin up. I am sure Willow will survive this unscathed. Your sister is a resourceful soul and is made of steel."

"She is." Georgina nodded. "She is. She will be fine. She will." Her words more trying to convince herself than him.

"I'll leave posthaste." Silas turned from her, his steps aimed for the wing that held his room, his thoughts calculating how long it would take to get to London and when he'd last seen Lord Fugal or his hideous cousins. Georgina could very well be right about Lord Fugal stealing Willow away.

He'd help where he could as far as the younger Constantine sister was concerned, for he didn't at all begrudge Willow for having a demon for a sister.

Plus, any assistance he gave would only help to solidify him as a trusted person in Georgina's eyes.

All the better to break her.

{ CHAPTER 9 }

Silas walked out of the stable after arriving back at Toften Hall. After finding Mr. Thatcher in London and convincing him to come search for Willow, Silas had to make one important stop, and then change out his horse in town before the ride back to the house party. Thatcher was at least a half hour in front of him.

So he wasn't surprised when he saw Thatcher striding down the hill toward the stables and his waiting horse. Silas tilted his hat to Thatcher, and Thatcher veered toward him.

"Atwell, I have a favor to ask of you."

Silas took a few steps toward Thatcher. "Name it."

Thatcher motioned toward his horse and didn't stop moving. Silas fell in step with him. "I am going in search for Willow and I need you to keep Georgina safe should Lord Fugal or one of his cousins reappear near her, whether here at Toften or in London."

"Watch over her? That I can do." His brows lifted. "But what is the concern over Lord Fugal?"

"The bastard has been trying to trap one of the sisters into a compromising position to force marriage and get to their dowries."

"That is low." Hearing it from Thatcher reaffirmed what Georgina had told him about the threat.

Thatcher nodded. "It is. And he has been quite vicious about it. So I need your help, because you know of the situation with Georgina and what she has been through."

Silas solemnly nodded. "I can help, but why not tell their uncle of the danger?"

"When I say Fugal and his cousins have been vicious, it means they will do anything to get what they want. I wouldn't put anything past them." Thatcher stopped and turned, looking directly at Silas. "The coachman."

Silas's eyebrows lifted. "You think they killed the coachman?"

"Aye. And to tell their uncle about the danger from Fugal would mean he would need to know about Georgina's affair with the coachman. And that is something I won't do to her."

Silas feigned surprise. "Wait, are you saying the babe was the coachman's? That driver that was killed in the stable?"

Thatcher's mouth pulled to a tight line and he nodded.

Silas whistled out a long sigh. "Hell."

"Yes." Thatcher started back toward his horse. "So I don't trust Fugal or his cousins anywhere near the family. Georgina must be protected from them at all costs."

"Then I am your servant on the matter."

Thatcher clapped him on the back of his shoulder. "Good man—thank you. It will assuage Willow's worry when I find her. She is, first and foremost, always concerned over Georgina."

Silas's lips pursed. "The sisters appear to have a bond that isn't easily broken."

"And never will be, I imagine." Thatcher shrugged his shoulders. "Though it is a lucky thing, to have someone that will unconditionally watch your back."

"Aye. It is." They both stopped as they reached Thatcher's horse tied to a hitching post. "Not to inquire into something that isn't my business, but I understand that to mean you intend to be the one that watches over Willow's back in the future?"

"I do. And not just her back." Simple. Direct. An explicit declaration.

Thatcher heaved himself up onto his horse.

Silas smiled. "Good luck with that."

"Just keep Georgina safe, especially if Lord Fugal or one of his cousins appears back here at the party. Don't let any of them within ten feet of her. Do whatever it takes."

"You have my word." Silas nodded, looking up at Thatcher on his horse. "God speed in finding Willow."

Thatcher tipped his hat to him and then set his horse on a fast pace along the drive that skirted around Toften Hall.

A smile played about Silas's lips as he watched Thatcher until he disappeared beyond the edge of the forest that surrounded the estate.

Interesting. An actual blessing on what he had been pondering doing for days—how to ruin every last sliver of Georgina's life and peace of mind.

Whatever it takes.

That could mean a number of things.

The answer of how to ruin Georgina suddenly there, in front of him.

The best way to watch over her would be to have her under his complete control, thereby fulfilling his promise to Thatcher.

A kidnapping it would be, then.

{ CHAPTER 10 }

"You have to come with me."

Georgina's shoulders straightened, her fingers holding the palette knife mixing red and yellow oil paints stilling.

Surrounded by easels and other ladies squinting at their canvases, they were in the sunny south drawing room which had been turned into an art room for the occasion of instruction from an artist from the Royal Academy.

The gentlemen at the house party had come and gone from the room throughout the morning and her face angled slightly toward Silas who had discreetly bent down behind her to whisper the words directly into her ear. He was already walking away from her.

She didn't care for the shiver of heat that ran across her shoulders at the heat of his breath on her neck. Shivers like that had been her downfall—had set into motion a cascade of horrors that had not only enveloped her, but had thrown Willow into danger as well.

Shivers were the last thing she wanted at the moment—or ever again.

After talking with Mr. Thatcher in the morning and sending him off to find Willow, she'd gone about the day, worry for her sister eating her up from the inside out. Yet she'd attempted to maintain a façade that displayed nothing amiss. Her aunt had declared Willow sick in her rooms, and that had kept questions about her sister's whereabouts from

circulating amongst the gossipmongers attending the house party.

It was easy to pretend now.

Her body had gone back to normal, the pain dissipating, the bleeding stopping—a small relief. So it was easy to look as though nothing was wrong when everything was. She'd lived in a web of lies for the last three months— she could make it a few more days until the house party ended.

Silas continued to move about the room, casually stopping to chat with the Brighton twins, and then to Lady Toften on his way out of the room. Just as he stepped into the hallway out of view from most everyone, he looked over his shoulder, pinning her with his stare.

Follow me now was the direct order demanded in that look.

The man was just as good an actor as she was.

Georgina waited a few more minutes before yawning loudly and she set her palette down, then tapped her fingers on the top edge of her canvas and stood up. "I am due for an afternoon rest, I believe," she said to no one in particular around her. The rest of the ladies were concentrating on their landscapes.

"Do not sleep for too long, dear, as we have dancing this eve and I would hate for you to be late to the ballroom," Lady Toften shouted out from behind her canvas across the way.

Georgina smiled at their hostess. "I will keep it to a reasonable time."

With one last glance at her atrocious sunset on her
canvas—the globe of the sun hung completely out of
proportion to the field and trees below it—she walked out
of the drawing room, wiping her paint-splattered fingers off
on her apron. No one had ever accused her of having actual
artistic ability. Not that it bothered her—she'd long since
accepted that fact and now just enjoyed mixing colors and
painting with wild strokes without rhyme or reason.

She walked down the dark hallway and it was as
though Silas had disappeared.

Until a hand reached out and grabbed her arm,
yanking her into the fourth room she passed, the billiards
room. Her balance gone, she slammed into the hard mass of
Silas.

Her hands landed on him to keep herself upright and
she looked up to his face. His hazel eyes looked down at her
with alarm.

"What is so urgent you needed to come in there and
order me about?" she asked, her voice a low whisper.

"Your sister."

That got her full attention. She pushed herself off
of him, never minding the paint on her fingers she was
probably smearing onto his dark coat. "What is it? What
has happened?"

"You have to come with me. I have a coach waiting."

"She has been found?"

Silas nodded. "And she needs you."

Her chest expanded in celebration that her sister had
been found, while dread seeped into her bones. There was

no telling what condition Willow would be in. Georgina turned toward the door. "I need to tell my aunt."

Silas grabbed her wrist before she escaped the room. "It is better that you do not. Better to handle this without her."

"Oh…" Georgina paused, her chest deflating as all the air left her.

Not Willow. Terror couldn't have been set upon her little sister. Not after she'd spent a lifetime protecting her. Not now. The one time it really mattered, when her sister really needed her, she had failed her. "Is she…is she alive?"

Silas nodded. "But best that you just come with me now."

Her hands went to the front of the apron covering her turquoise day dress. "Of course, of course, let me just change—"

"There isn't time for that. We need to leave. Now."

Georgina nodded.

"Come, we'll slip out the side door." He grabbed her hand and led her through the dark shadows of the empty billiards room and toward the door that led outside to the gardens.

Two hours later, with her hands wringing in the coach the entire time, Georgina still had no idea what had happened to her sister. Silas would tell her nothing.

In fact, Silas had been tight-lipped through most of the ride.

Not that she could blame him.

The poor man had unwittingly gotten entangled with the spectacle of her life when he'd found her in the woods. And then she had asked him to fetch Mr. Thatcher to help

find her sister. She had been one problem after another
for Silas. None of which he had responsibility for, yet the
problems had been heaped upon him and he had taken all
of it with grace and kindness she didn't deserve.

He had helped her, no questions asked, time and again.

She studied him across the carriage. His stare had been
set solidly out the window for the last hours, though he
didn't appear to be actually watching the scenery.

Lost in thought. Probably pondering what a bane to his
existence she was.

But heaven above, he was handsome. His dark hair
always had a tousled look about it, like the wind was always
having its way, inside or out. The hard cuts of his nose,
cheekbones and jawline. Almost so hard that one might feel
a flicker of fear for the warriors he must be descended from.
But then set in the middle, his hazel eyes that held rings
of brown interrupted with sparks of blue that looked like
lightning exploding.

That was what had drawn her to him in the first place.
His unusual eyes. Eyes that were kind. Intelligent. Honest.

Eyes that looked at her with heat and lust and made
the bottom of her stomach quiver.

Such magnetic eyes that she had entertained the
thought—even knowing it could never happen with Leroy's
babe in her belly—of possibly making a match with him. A
dream she would never attain, so she had tried to squelch it
the moment it had popped into her head.

She looked down at her lap.

So many mistakes.

So. Many. Damn. Mistakes.

She cleared her throat, looking up at him. "How much farther is it?"

He glanced at her, then set his stare back out the window like he was truly noticing their surroundings. "Not but another five minutes and we should reach the turn-off."

She nodded, her left thumb and forefinger twisting harder around the tip of her right forefinger. So hard and for so long, the cuticle had worn down and tore, smearing little spots of blood onto her nail.

No matter. Silas would think the color was just from the paint on her fingers from earlier.

She drew in a deep breath as the coach turned, the deep bumps in the roadway jarring her back and forth. So much so, she had to set both hands onto the cushions on either side of her to remain upright. Silas, on the other hand, took the bumps in stride, his thick body absorbing each bump, his posture never changing.

Willow had to be all right. She *had* to be.

And if Willow wasn't?

Well, then, Georgina would just have to make her so with nothing but sheer will.

Georgina leaned to the side, looking out the window to see if she recognized the destination. At first, nothing but woods of ancient oaks and evergreens towering beside the lane were evident, but then weathered grey stones came into view. A castle surged up from the ground, probably three hundred years old. Turrets topped four towers that anchored the castle in all directions. Formidable. Brooding.

How in the hell had Willow ended up here?

"Silas—please—what happened? I need to know what I'm walking into. I need to ready myself."

A pained look slipped across his face with a slight shake of his head. "I don't think I can prepare you."

With that, the bottom dropped out of her stomach and her limbs turned to jelly.

No.

Weakness was not an option at the moment.

Whatever happened to Willow, they would get through it together, like they always had.

Georgina set her hand flat on her belly, pressing inward, trying to stop her stomach from twisting about in fear, and she looked to Silas. "Thank you. Thank you for everything. For not only this, but for finding me in the woods. I know we have not had a moment in private to talk since then, but I thank you for your help, for your silence, for your honor when the situation had little honor in it."

His lips pulled inward, his hazel eyes going sharp for a short second as he stared at her. Then he nodded. "You are welcome. I won't say that I was happy to help, but I do count it fortunate that it was I that found you and was able to help."

The coach stopped and the footman opened the door to the carriage.

Silas alighted, then turned back to help her down the step.

Not releasing her hand, he led her toward the front door and opened it.

Odd, that he would boldly walk into someone else's home, but before she had a chance to ask about it, his long

strides ate up the distance in the wide foyer and along a hallway that led deep into the castle. Her hand still encased in his, she had to run just to stay up with his speed.

He stopped at a thick wooden door, darkened with time, and opened it, pointing inward to the circular staircase it led to. He looked back over his shoulder at her. "She's up here in a room."

"What? Up there?" Georgina looked upward, but could only see the ancient stones of the staircase curving above her. Desperation set her hand along Silas's back and she pushed him up the stairs. "Then we need to get up there."

Her legs were screaming for relief after countless spins upward along the staircase, and she was panting by the time Silas stopped at the top of the stairs.

He veered out of the staircase into a small landing area with one door. He opened it, and she rushed past him into the room.

"Willow?" Her look went frantic as she searched every corner in the room for her sister. An old armoire. A creaky tester bed with wood splintering on the headboard and a frayed canopy of cloth so faded she couldn't judge the color of it. A small desk and chair. The only things in the room. No Willow.

The door clicked closed behind her.

The sound eerily ominous in the silence. She spun around.

Silas stood in front of the door, his look set on her. "Willow is not here."

She stepped toward him. "Not here? Where did she go? Is she below?"

The right side of his mouth pulled back. "No. She was never here."

"Never here?" Her eyebrows drew together.

"Honestly, this was the only way I could think of to get you here."

"Where is here?"

"My estate. Yarstone."

She stilled, the hairs along her head spiking, her words coming out slow, pointed. "Why did you need to get me here?"

"I promised Thatcher I would keep you safe. This is the best place for that."

"Keep me safe? Safe from what?" Her hand went over her mouth. "Willow—she's in dire trouble, isn't she? Did Jack say something? If my sister is in trouble, I need to find her. I need to find her now."

She rushed forth, trying to push past him.

He threw out an arm that cut her off at the waist, stopping her from getting past him. "No, you can't protect her."

She shoved off of him, taking a step backward, her voice rising. "I've been protecting Willow my whole life—there is no one better to do so. You need to help me find her."

"No."

"No?" Her arm swung out about her. "So you think to keep me here?"

"Yes." He nodded. "Locked up, since I don't know another way to keep you safely in place."

Her jaw went so slack it was hard to form words. "You're going to lock me in here?"

"Yes."

"But you—you cannot do that."

"I can."

"But—"

"Tell me, Georgina, what is the first thing you would do the minute I left this room?" His arms crossed over his chest, his stance massive and looming in front of the door. A door that was her only escape.

Her jaw shifted back and forth, her look darting from him to the door handle as she measured her chances of getting past him.

No chance.

Her look crept up to his face. A face now set in stone. A face she refused to let cow her. "I would run out of here as fast as I could and scour the countryside for Willow."

"Exactly. So this is the solution. Thatcher knew it. I knew it."

"What gives you and Jack any say in how or if I'm protected?"

"The very fact that if we don't, you would likely fall to great harm or be killed. Or did the murder of that coachman slip by you unnoticed?"

She hiccupped a breath, his words a punch to her gut. Of all things, Leroy's death had not gone unnoticed. His death had kicked off everything that had happened to her in the last week, including this man's unfortunate entanglement with her.

Turning away from him, she walked over to the lone window in the room. High above the ground. Nothing but a small patch of open land and then forest out her view.

"So, you're locking me in a tower. How original."

He didn't move from his spot in front of the door. "This is for your own good."

Her own good?

What good could come of this? She should be out there, looking for Willow herself at this very moment. She never should have trusted him. Trusted Jack.

And then the full consequences of what this was set into her mind. What this was beyond Willow. What this would mean, disappearing from the Toften estate for heaven only knew how long.

She spun around toward him and her eyes narrowed, instant hatred spewing out at this overbearing ogre of a man. "You just bloody well ruined me. I disappear without a trace for even a day and I am ruined. You just ruined my whole life."

"It's better than being dead, little dragon."

"Says the man that just took my entire future away from me."

His top lip curled into a snarl. "Believe me, with your inheritance, nothing could ruin you. Any man with coffers in need of plumping will still be in line for you, no matter your state of ruin."

There it was. And he was shoving her nose in it.

The one thing that had haunted her since they'd come to London for the season. There wasn't a man on this

blasted isle that wanted her for anything more than her inheritance.

She spun back toward the window, a heavy breath expelling from her lungs. "Not the right men."

"Oh? What are the right men? Your lover, the coachman?"

Her look snapped over her shoulder to him. "How do you know that?"

Silas shrugged. "It wasn't hard to deduce. Your hysterical reaction when he was found dead. You ran out of the barn in a mad flurry." His stare sliced into her. "You carried his babe, so he must have been the exact match you were looking for."

"You could never have deduced all of that."

"Except you just verified the fact."

"You don't know what you think you do."

"No?"

"No." She shook her head, her glare trying to split him in two. "He wasn't the right man."

His eyebrows lifted.

He didn't believe her. But she was already past being worried about what this dung heap thought of her.

How had she ever found Silas handsome? Ever found him witty and charming? Ever thought to depend upon him?

How did she—again and again—fall for men with cores of misery?

She spun away from him, facing the window. "When do I get to leave?"

"When it is safe. I will let you know."

"So I'm a captive here?" She couldn't bear to look at him as she asked the question.

"Call it what you will."

"Silas? Silas? Silas?" A sudden voice, low and booming, echoed up the staircase and through the heavy oak door.

She glanced back at him as he looked over his shoulder.

His glare jerked back to her. "As I was saying, call it what you will, but you are not leaving."

"Silas? Silas? The ass." Muffled sounds of boots clomping on stairs made way into the room. "Lord Atwell? Where in the hell are you?"

With a sigh, Silas turned toward the door. "You will forgive me. I must attend to my guests."

He slipped out of the room and slammed the door closed, most likely for effect.

A key clinked the lock into place.

Point made.

{ CHAPTER 11 }

The window was old.

No matter how she shoved at it, she couldn't get it to open. The hinges on the left side meant the curved-topped window should swing open inward. But it was stuck in place. Time had warped the entire leaded glass window into place.

Her palm slammed against the frame of the window.

She needed it open, because if she was right about what she thought she saw out of the corner of the window, she still had a chance to get out of here. A chance she had to take.

Georgina went over to the small desk on the far wall and gently set it onto its side. Unnecessary care, for what she was about to do.

Thank the heavens she'd been wearing sturdy boots today. She lifted her right foot, aligning her heel over one of the legs of the desk, and then smashed it downward.

Miss.

The vibrations from her heel hitting the floor shot up her leg and gave her pause. But the desk wasn't going to beat her.

She lifted her foot again, smashing it down. Wood splintered and she yanked the leg free.

Going over to the window, she tried to wedge in along the edge of the window the sharp, splintered side of the leg

to pry the pane of glass open. The dry wood split, weak. No success.

She sighed. Such a pretty window.

Only one option. She spun around the length of wood in her hand and pulled it back, then slammed the fat tip of it into the glass, shattering the window.

She'd hoped to avoid it, but ruining the window was her only option. Winter was still five months away so she didn't have to worry about freezing drafts. And if she was still stuck in this room by then…well…she'd just have to jump straight out of the window at that point.

Knocking out the lead and the sharp shards of glass away from the wooden frame, she crunched on pieces that had shattered inside the room as she leaned out of the window and looked to her right.

There.

Yes.

The edge stones of a parapet on a battlement were just down and to the right. Straight out from the window, the drop was long and sheer, but if she could somehow swing herself onto that parapet, she could escape down and out of this blasted place.

If she dropped, she'd be dead.

But if she stayed in here and Willow died and she did nothing to save her, she wouldn't want to live anyway.

She just had to be smart about how she went about it.

Turning back toward the room, she looked around. The armoire was ancient, a heavy box with no legs. She went to it and opened it to find it was empty.

She spun around. The bed had chunky legs and it looked sturdy enough.

Moving to it, she bent over, her hands on the board that ran along the foot of the four-post bed, and she tried to shove it out of place. It squeaked across the old floorboards, but just barely.

With every one of her muscles straining, she spent the next ten minutes shoving the heavy bed across the floor. It scraped the entire time, and it was a miracle Silas didn't come back into the room at the sound.

When the bottom of the bed was close to the window, she stripped the bed of its worn coverlet and sheets, testing each stretch of fabric for strength, then splitting them the best she could by starting a tear with her teeth and then ripping them in half lengthwise. Tying them all together, she cobbled together a makeshift rope.

Not the best rope. But she tested it as she went, throwing it over the top railing of the bed and hanging on it with her weight. It held.

Tying one end of it around the bottom leg of the bed closest to the window, she threw the rope out the window, watching to see how far it unfurled.

Just a little short.

Taking off her paint-stained apron, she pulled the makeshift rope into the room, added her apron to the end of it and tested it along the outer wall once more.

It should work, even tied around her waist.

She brought the rope in, secured it around her waist, then threw the loop of the excess rope out the window. Curling into a ball, she moved onto the ledge of the window and balanced on her toes as she gave the rope one

last tug against its tie to the bed, carefully watching the knot she'd made. It didn't shift. If anything, it pulled tighter, locking in place.

Her mouth dry, she tried to swallow but found it impossible to do so, the fear creeping up into her.

She closed her eyes, setting her chin on her chest.

Faith. She just had to have faith.

She double-wrapped the rope around both of her hands so she could hold one hand in place while letting the other down. Over and over, and slowly she could make her way down.

Or so she hoped.

She dropped one foot off the ledge, the toe of her boot searching about the grey stone for a foothold. There. The tiniest of spots.

Her hands gripping tight to the rope, the blood in her veins on fire, she dropped her other foot off the edge of the windowsill.

Heaven help her, the rope held. She pushed the flat of her boot onto the stone and curled her body toward the wall.

Little by little, she worked herself down the side of the tower. The muscles in her arms near to popping, sweat broke out across her brow.

Downward until she reached the end of the rope.

Now she just had to shift a bit to the left.

Her knuckles scraped against the weathered stone, trailing streaks of blood.

Inch by inch until she heard fabric ripping above her and she dropped for half a second before the strength of the rope caught her again.

No time for slow.

Her feet scrambled, pushing her to the left, and her toes reached for the top of the turret just as more fabric tore. Her other foot found landing and she pushed off the wall until she was balancing on the stone parapet.

Her hands shaking, she tore at the knot around her belly until it loosened and then jumped down from the perch on the wall onto the walkway of the battlement.

Doors in both directions.

Crouching low so no one would see her across the open expanse above the battlement, she moved as fast as she could away from the tower.

Luck was on her side, for the door farthest from the tower was open and led to a staircase inside.

Her feet light, she scrambled down the steps until she found an ancient, warped door she had to smash her right shoulder into so it would budge.

The door slammed open and she stumbled out, losing her balance on the slick grass. She crashed directly into a hard stomach.

Stomach. White shirt. Black and grey brocade waistcoat. Hands set just above his hips.

She looked up.

Silas.

Silas seething.

She shoved off of him and jabbed a step backward. Another. Her back hit the planks of the door she'd slammed open.

"I didn't think you had it in you."

Her look darted about, frantic.

Silas and no one else. After all of that—after dropping out of a bloody window—she wasn't about to give up. If she could reach the woods she could lose him.

She sprinted to her right, making it a good eight strides before an arm slammed around her waist, stopping her motion, and her feet flew out from under her.

Blasted skirt. Blasted legs of his that were far too long.

She clawed at the arm clamped about her waist. "You bastard, let me go."

"I'm not the bastard." He picked her up far too easily and slung her over his shoulder, the top edge of his collarbone digging painfully into her belly. "And I cannot let you leave. Not yet."

He walked toward the castle, his arm locked across the back of her thighs, holding her in place.

For a moment she considered beating his back to let her go, but then disregarded the urge. It wouldn't work. Not with him. He wasn't about to set her down until he deemed it was time, and to fight it would just waste energy she didn't have. Mangle the last bits of self-respect she possessed.

She suffered his shoulder jabbing into her belly with every step as he walked through the castle and up the main set of stairs in the middle of the structure. Or at least that's what she assumed with her limited view through her hair falling about and shielding most of her head.

Two flights of stairs upward and he strode into a room a number of steps down a hallway to the left.

The room was dark—dark colors all around—and then he moved into a connecting room and she was suddenly flying through the air as he tossed her off his shoulder.

She landed on a bed, her arms sprawling out and her legs askew, her skirt crumpled up onto her thighs.

She scrambled on the bed, quick to shove her skirts down and into place around her legs. But she couldn't stand up, for Silas was standing at the edge of the bed between her legs.

The seething look on his face hadn't abated. If anything, it was worse, a vein along his left temple throbbing as he glared down at her.

"Are you stark mad, Georgina? You could have broken your neck with that stunt."

Her lip pulled back in a snarl. "Better a broken neck than to be under your capture."

He smirked. "That can be arranged, if that is truly how you would like this to play out."

Her breath puffed out, stolen from her chest.

He wouldn't. He couldn't.

But the look on his face sent a shiver down her spine.

Hatred. Pure molten hatred.

She'd never thought Silas a danger to her—not physically—but in that moment, he looked like he'd flay the skin from her body.

This wasn't about keeping her safe from Lord Fugal and his cousins. This wasn't about stealing her away to force her into marriage and gain her inheritance.

None of those things.

For the loathing seeping from him, this was about something she didn't understand the first thing about.

Her mouth clamped shut for once, recognizing exactly what was on his face.

She'd always wanted to believe in the fairytale. That her sister would marry and then she would meet a wonderful man and he would court her with poetry and sweet words and stolen kisses. That they would marry in the summer surrounded by flowers at her uncle's estate. That they would take a year for a grand tour, mostly so she could see the art in Rome, before returning to England and she would birth a boy first, and then a girl, and then two more of each. Then she would die a plump old lady surrounded by her love and her children and countless grandchildren.

It was all there, just waiting for her to take.

And now it was gone.

All of it.

All because she'd looked at this man in front of her and thought him more than he was. Thought him honorable. Thought him handsome. Thought him honest.

She never could judge people. That was Willow's forte. She was cursed with only seeing what she wanted to in the people around her. Only the good. A hopeless dreamer when there was so much bad in this world.

It hurt her soul, down to her toes, that she could be so very, stupidly, wrong about all of it. Not once, but twice.

First Leroy. Now Silas.

He stared at her for a long moment before he scoffed a laugh, then shook his head and turned away from her.

Yet keeping her mouth shut was never her strong suit. Someone attacked, she fought back. She always did. It was how she'd protected Willow all these years. "You really are evil, aren't you? You had everyone fooled. Everyone. Me included. But you are nothing but the devil himself."

He looked back to her. "I'm not the evil one in this story you are telling yourself, Georgina. Far from it. I am merely the player tasked with setting consequences upon those that deserve it."

"A player that is judge and executioner?"

"Exactly."

The snarl on his lips, his hazel eyes vibrating in contempt, told her everything she needed to know.

She was never getting out of here.

{ CHAPTER 12 }

Her breath heaving in indignation, Georgina glared up at him, the last tattered threads of her defiance not allowing her to back down.

Her cheeks flush, her blue eyes on fire, her hair tousled in all directions.

She could have fallen. Could have *died*.

And all he wanted to do in that moment was sink his cock deep into her. Pound her into the bed, taking from her everything her body had to give. Devour every one of her screams as her body tightened around his shaft, making her come so hard she had no energy left to fight him, to hate him for stealing her away from Toften Hall.

He blinked, momentarily stunned at the flash of that image in his mind.

Where in the hell had that thought come from?

He swallowed, looking up from Georgina splayed out on the bed, to the motif painted upon the curved ceiling. Cherubs in six panels, flitting about with flowers and sea serpents and winged horses. He always hated those cherubs. Always reminding him of what he would never have with Josie.

He took another step away from Georgina, his boot heel thudding hard on the carpet.

The thought of stripping her bare and sliding into her had no right to exist in his head. It had to be that she was

in his bed. That was the only reason his mind would veer there.

She was his prisoner, at least until he was sure she'd been ruined in the eyes of all those that loved her.

And then what would be left for her? Spinsterhood with a life of regrets. Or a pitiful marriage to a money-grubbing wastrel.

Either were too good for the conniving witch.

Yet still, he couldn't kill her. Even with what she'd taken from him.

So ruin her. Ruin her for real.

That thought snaked about in his head, trying to entice him toward a darkness he wasn't about to tread into. An evil, tempting voice that had to be the reason he was suddenly imagining ramming his cock into her.

He wouldn't accept any other reason.

"Why do you hate me?" Her voice curled out at him like a snare, biting and dangerous.

"Why do you think I hate you?" He took a moment to force his features into blankness, then set an impassive gaze upon her. "I just spent a significant amount of time during the last week wooing you."

"Except that wasn't you. Clearly, that man at Toften Hall was a very different person than the man that is now standing in this room."

His shoulders lifted. "Same man. The only thing that has changed is your perception."

"So you hated me for a fortnight, yet attended to me most religiously? Filling my dance card? Positioning yourself to partner with me at cards again and again? Walking with me on each and every outing? Helping me in the woods when you found me bloody and tortured and you had every right to walk away and pretend you never saw me?"

His look shifted to the window, refusing to look at her. He had done those things. He'd done all of them—save for helping her in the woods—before he knew what a wicked Judas she was.

He wasn't about to tell her he knew she'd had his wife killed. Let her twist in the wind, searching endlessly for answers.

That way promised madness.

And what he wouldn't do to drive her into the mad house.

He walked across his room and motioned for her to follow. He lightened his voice into feigned kindness. "Come with me." He pointed forward. "Come, look out the window."

Her eyes narrowed at him. She hesitated for moment before she finished righting her skirts and slid off the bed, joining him at the window. Her gaze set forward, she wouldn't look up at him.

"Look out, look around." He swept and arc with his forefinger at the window. "There is nothing. Nothing to swing onto. No way to lower yourself down, no matter how many sheets you tie together. Only a drop."

He turned fully toward her, studying her profile as her look shifted downward toward the ground outside. "So jump if you're going to jump. The window opens easily. Just know that at this height, you'll probably not die right away at impact. You'll break a slew of bones and die a slow,

agonizing death, blood filling up your insides, and you'll wish you had just jumped from the tower when you had the chance."

She pulled back, her breath quickening.

"Your feet on the floor, then?"

She nodded, real fear flickering in her haunting blue eyes. Eyes that finally lifted to him. "I don't understand any of this—why are you doing this to me?"

"Honestly?"

She swallowed hard, her throat bobbing. "Please."

"It's what you deserve."

Her look dropped from him for a breath, then lifted to pin him. "So, this doesn't have anything to do with Willow?"

"No."

"Then it has to do with what I did, how you found me in the woods, my lack of morals?" Her voice caught on the last of the question.

"The last thing I care about is who you've had in your bed and what you do there." His cock twitched as he said the words. His cock knew a lie when it heard one, even if his mind didn't.

She reeled slightly, her heels dragging backward until she landed heavily in a wingback chair set by the cold fireplace.

Her face had turned ashen, her hands starting to shake. "I don't…I don't know what I did to you that was so grievous. Please, is it…is it my inheritance you're after?"

"I couldn't care less about your money."

"Then what?" Her look lifted to him, her eyes starting to water, sending a bright sheen across her light blue irises. "What did I do? I can rectify it. I can. If I only knew what I did. I'm sorry. Sorry for what, I don't know. But I am sorry for the hate I see in your eyes. I will rectify it however I can, just please, let me go. You cannot think to keep me here forever."

"I can do whatever I damn well please."

A flicker of motion and he looked down. A drop of blood had just splattered onto the Axminster carpet, seeping into the worn and faded fibers.

Blood? What the hell?

The second he'd heard the glass in her room break, he'd run outside, expecting to see her broken body on the ground. It wasn't. But then he'd heard an odd scraping sound coming from the room. So he'd waited, watching the window. By the time the rope of sheets was tossed out the window, he knew he was too late to run up to the tower and stop her from whatever foolishness she was about to embark upon. In the next minute, she had been crawling up onto the windowsill and snaking her way down the side of the tower.

Nothing to do but watch.

In all honesty, he'd held his breath as she dangled far above the ground, for heaven only knew how sturdy that sheet she'd fashioned into a rope had been. In his gut, no matter what she had done, he hadn't wanted her to fall.

And now there was blood?

He pointed to the carpet. "Where is that blood coming from?"

Her eyebrows drew together. "What blood?"

"From under your skirt—along your leg?"

"I don't…" She shook her head and looked down. She froze for a moment and then grabbed the skirts in her lap, rearranging them about her legs to fully cover her feet. "It is fine. I am sure it is nothing."

He charged toward her and yanked up her skirt.

A shard of glass was embedded into her calf, blood running from the wound. Not just a trickle—a steady stream.

"You knew this was stuck in your flesh?"

"No." She blanched, her head starting to sway back and forth. "I only just noticed the pain when you mentioned it."

She looked down at her leg, then instantly averted her gaze, her breath speeding, her entire torso falling into a sway that started to circle, like she couldn't quite keep her body straight.

He pushed her skirt fully onto her lap. "You have a long shard of glass embedded into your leg. How could you not feel that? Feel the blood?" He grabbed her ankle and lifted her leg straight so he could see the wound better.

"I…I…I…" She looked down at her leg once more. "I…I did not—" She slumped over in the chair, dead to the world.

A fainter.

Bloody hell.

She could drop herself out of a tower window with nothing but a slip of fabric keeping her from certain death, but a little bit of blood and she was done for.

Funny that she hadn't had this reaction to the blood in the woods when she had lost the babe. For a moment, he considered that she was faking her reaction to the blood on her leg. Then again, she clearly hadn't been in her right mind in the woods, and she had slipped in and out of consciousness numerous times that night.

Silas seethed in a long breath through clenched teeth.

Still holding her ankle, he reached out and pulled toward him an ottoman that was close to the hearth. He set her outstretched foot onto the stool and walked over to the washbasin, dunking a washcloth into the bowl after pouring water into it.

Cradling the washbasin, he moved back to her and stared at her face for a long moment. With her eyes closed, she looked almost peaceful if not for the line creased in the center of her brow. An agitated angel.

No. An agitated devil playing the angel.

He had to remember that, no matter how innocent she looked.

She was a devil that had to pay.

With a heaved sigh, he set the washbasin on the carpet and dropped onto his knees in front of her calf.

Just below her knee, the shard of glass was intact enough that he could grab the edge of it and pluck it from her flesh. He flung it into the fireplace, the glass clinking and shattering on the iron grate.

As he wrung out the cloth above the basin, he investigated her skin. It was possible that a smaller shard or two had broken off from the larger piece and embedded

deeper into her skin, but he had pulled it clean out from what he could tell. It looked like there was only the one cut.

Little slivers of glass would fester in the wound, cutting her from the inside, and for a moment, he considered leaving the gash as it was.

But he couldn't do it.

His job for the last ten years was to protect people, not to harm them.

Doing in the coachman for killing Josie had been easy. But he was finding it difficult to harden himself against Georgina.

Only a demon witch down to her bones could have such an effect.

He leaned closer to the wound, washing the blood away from the gash, then pulling the flesh open wide and dripping water deep into the wound to see if there were any glitters from any rogue shards catching the light. He washed out the one shard he found.

When he was assured no more glass was in the cut, he went to his chest of drawers and pulled free some linen strips he kept in the room—usually used to wrap his own wounds.

Reassuming his position in front of Georgina's leg, he started to wrap the linen strip around her leg several times.

A sudden gasp filled the room and Georgina shot straight upward, knocking her knee into Silas's nose.

"What the deuce?" she spat out, her eyes wild as she looked about the room. Her face suddenly fell. "Oh." She looked at him, then her leg. "Oh."

Silas pinched the bridge of his nose. Not broken, but it would ache for a while. "Oh, indeed." He grabbed her ankle and placed it back on the ottoman.

"Sorry. I didn't mean to knock your nose. Or to faint." She glanced down at her leg, her face in a squint as though she didn't want to look but had to. "I don't do well with the sight of blood. Never have."

His brows lifted. "Are you going to be sick?" She looked paler than she had before she saw the blood.

She shook her head. "No. I will be fine." She pointed to her leg, her voice warbling. "Do you want…I can wrap it myself."

He glanced at her face. He'd never seen anyone so close to retching but holding it in. "I'll do it."

Relief flooded her face and he had to look away.

The last thing he wanted from her was gratefulness.

He unfurled the wrap that was now half hanging off the wound and busied himself rewrapping her calf.

She let him, silent for a minute before her voice interrupted him. "Thank you—I know you don't want to be doing this, because—for whatever the reason—you truly hate me." Her leg twitched under his hands. "So thank you, but know I usually don't need help like this."

He didn't look up from her calf. "You're telling me you don't have an army of servants ready to do your bidding?"

"If I needed it, yes, my uncle would make it happen. But I have never been like that. I don't like people around me. Around my sister."

"Why not?"

She cleared her throat, fidgeting as his hands brushed against her leg. "You know about Willow's oddity?"

"I do."

"I presumed as much. Everyone seems to know." Her lips pulled inward for a long moment. "That's why. I don't like the gossip. I don't like how it affects her. How it crushes her soul, little bit by little bit, one whispered word at a time. It crushes her soul, and that, in turn, crushes my soul."

He nodded. Her sister had been dealt a raw deal from her maker. And Silas did have to admit that if Georgina had one redeeming quality about her, it was how she protected her younger sister from all that society threw at them.

"So I don't like to depend on people. I never did."

Yet she had.

She had let Josie into her life—had hired his wife to protect her. Befriended her. Then betrayed her. Killed her.

He yanked the ends of the linen wrap, tying off the knot far too tight. "And now you have no one left to depend on now that your precious coachman is gone?"

"What? No." She leaned down, slipping a finger beneath his knot and trying to loosen it. "And he wasn't my precious."

Silas leaned back on his heels. "You didn't love him?"

She looked up at him. "No. Far from it. He was a mistake. And then he was my only option."

"Your only option?" Silas stilled, his gaze slicing into her. This was news to him. "You were going to elope with him?"

She shrugged.

"If he was a mistake, then why elope with him?"

"I loved the baby inside of me. That was enough. I would have done anything to protect it."

His stomach tightened as she said the words.

That was why.

Why she'd had Josie killed. Josie was the one thing keeping a ruffian like that coachman away from Georgina. It made such perfect sense.

And it was the final nail in her coffin.

His jaw set hard and he pushed himself off the floor, looming over her, barely bridled rage in his voice. "Be well aware there is no one that will protect you now."

She scoffed and turned her head away from him, staring at the empty fireplace. "I am quickly coming to realize that."

{ CHAPTER 13 }

He walked out of the room without another word.

The clinking of a key in the lock on the door telling her nothing had changed.

She was still his prisoner.

Georgina sat there, in the silence of his absence, staring at the cold fireplace for long minutes.

What in the hell had just happened to her life?

Yesterday she had been begging Silas to ride to London to collect Jack to help find Willow. Her sister had been the one in dire danger.

And now...now she didn't know what was happening.

If Silas meant to kill her or rape her, he would have done so already.

If he meant to ruin her so he could force a marriage, he probably would have admitted to it, for his words since arriving at this castle were honest, the best she could tell.

Then again, what did she know about a man's honesty?

What she did understand was that Silas didn't want her. He didn't want to look at her, the hatred pouring off of him almost too much to bear.

She had done something, but the only thing she could possibly imagine was that once he'd discovered she was a fallen woman, he had grown to despise her.

Maybe that was it.

Maybe he had looked at her as a possibility for a solid match, and then he had discovered in the worst possible way she was soiled goods.

And now he was just making sure the world knew she was a compromised woman. Maybe that's what was driving him. He truly did want to see her ruined as she deserved.

Her head snapped to the side, her eyes studying the room she was in. It was spacious. A master suite if ever there was one. But the furnishings were minimal. A heavy, ancient four-post bed that had carvings of lions and vines etched deep into the headboard and twisted columns. A bed that probably hadn't been moved from its spot in two hundred years.

A dark blue silk coverlet covered the bed. The newest thing in the room.

A wide armoire sat against the wall opposite her. Also heavy and ancient, with the same elaborate carvings, but the doors of it were askew, as if they had fallen off and not been reattached properly.

A newer secretary desk with rows of identical drawers lining downward was positioned just to the left of the window with the faded blue drapes. A big desk with lines of inlaid walnut, it was probably from a study, not the usual kind placed in a bedroom. A few pieces of paper sat atop the desk in front of a quill and inkwell set.

The grey stone walls of the room were bare. When she'd been in other rooms in halls or castles similar to this, they always had tapestries or plaster walls in front of the stone. While not nearly as old as this castle, all the rooms in Grovewick Abbey on her family's main estate were cozy and warm, no matter that many of the rooms were as cavernous as this one.

The drafts in this bedroom would set a constant chill into one's bones during the winter.

All of it sorely needed updating. From what little she had seen, only the bones of this castle were showing, none of the meat that would make this home an actual home.

Though maybe that was exactly what was intended here. Silas's soul was reflected in his surroundings. Maybe this was who Silas really was—bones, sharp and pointy with none of the meat that would make him a whole person, none of the compassion, the kindness, the honor that she had thought she'd seen in him.

The ache in her leg from the glass cutting her had stopped throbbing enough to offer her a bit of energy. Energy she couldn't waste.

Best to know one's enemy.

For she had to get it in her head that Silas was the enemy. Not the dashing lord she'd met at Toften Hall.

She checked over the cut on her leg. He'd wrapped it well enough, if too tight, and she could only see a tinge of red seeping through the top layer of the binding.

Why tend to the wound if he hated her? Why not let the wound get infected and rot and cause her misery? For that was what his goal appeared to be.

She swallowed hard, not able to stomach adjusting the bandage, so she pushed her skirt over her leg and stood, then moved throughout the room.

This Spartan existence couldn't possibly be all there was to the man?

She started at the bed, her hand running along the coverlet, and wafts of Silas hit her nostrils. Definitely his bed. She would recognize that mixture of sandalwood and spice and evergreen anywhere. She had always thought he smelled like a forest, like the scent of him came from bathing in the air of the trees. This was absolutely his room.

She moved to the armoire, creaking open one of the damaged doors, and she peeked inside. Several dark coats were hung within, along with trousers and white lawn shirts. Not nearly enough to fill the massive wardrobe. She leaned in and sniffed. Still his scent.

She had to wedge the door upward to get it to close back into place, then moved to the chest of drawers that sat beneath the pitcher of water. Linen bandages. Some short splints. Tweezers and scissors, curved needles and threads.

This wasn't the man's first encounter with a bloody wound.

She walked past the bed, going to the desk by the window. The paper atop was blank, not even an insignia imprinted along any of the edges.

She rummaged through the drawers on the left side of the desk. More ink, quills, paper. Onto the right side.

Red wax and a wooden-handled seal. She lifted the metal stamp, turning it over to look at the design etched into the metal.

It was a mess of swirls, so many that she couldn't make out what it said.

Grabbing the quill next to the inkwell, she dipped the tip into the ink, then dropped splotches of the ink onto the seal, using her finger to smear the ink onto the raised ridges.

She turned it over and pressed it onto the paper, then lifted it carefully so as to not smear the ink.

What was that? It looked vaguely familiar.

Setting the seal back in the drawer, she leaned down, squinting as she looked at the emblem on the paper.

Letters. Curved.

Guardians of the Bones.

Hell.

There was no way Silas was a guardian. Impossible.

He was a marquess. A respected lord. A gentleman. Everyone at Lady Toften's house party knew him.

It was impossible he was a guardian.

Miss Sanders, the woman their Great-Aunt Simone had suggested they hire to protect her and Willow months ago from untoward advances by gentlemen of the *ton*, had been a guardian from the Guardians of the Bones. One of the best, their great-aunt had said. And Great-Aunt Simone had impeccable judgement—she had the uncanny ability to judge a person's character in the first thirty seconds. She'd never been wrong. That was where Willow had gotten her ability to read people.

Great-Aunt Simone had suggested Miss Sanders as the person to guard them and she had been right in her assessment of the woman.

But now Silas was a guardian as well? It didn't make sense. Great-Aunt Simone had said the Guardians of the Bones could be trusted unequivocally, but now Silas was one of them? No. Impossible.

Except. What if it was possible?

If he was a guardian, then what she saw today wasn't him. Not the real him.

It didn't make sense.

The guardians helped people. She knew it firsthand. Miss Sanders had not only been an excellent protector; she had become a dear friend as well. Georgina still missed her terribly, every single day.

Georgina had to close her eyes tight, blanking out all thoughts of Miss Sanders from her mind. Blanking out what she had witnessed. Blanking out that entire horrible day.

She exhaled a breath and shook her head as she stood straight, opening her eyes to stare at the emblem on the paper.

The guardians helped people.

They didn't kidnap them.

Maybe Silas had stolen the seal?

Or maybe he *was* a guardian, or had been at some point.

If so, there was honor in him. However little it had been whittled down to, but it still had to be there.

Whatever had prompted the change in him, she could undo it. Silas had liked her, cared for her—she could see that plain as day in the first week of the house party. She hadn't imagined it. She just needed to get him back to that place. And she wasn't above using every method at her disposal to get him to look at her like that again.

With lust.

Lust could turn back into like and he would let her go. Bring her back to Toften Hall before too much damage was done to her reputation.

She glanced out the window. The last streaks of purple were leaving the sky, twilight descending. It was still early into the evening hours. She could be back at Toften Hall and into her bed before sunrise.

The damage would be minimal. It had to be.

A clink into the lock in the door and Georgina spun around. The heavy oak door swung open.

A tarnished silver platter with bread and meat atop it preceded Silas into the room. He stepped fully in and closed the door behind him. "Food to keep you alive."

His words cut off as he walked across the room toward her and clanked the platter on top of the desk.

Apparently, he wasn't going to add on the "*for now,*" that his comment begged for.

About to turn toward her, he stopped, stilling, his stare on the paper next to the platter.

Georgina winced. She hadn't had time to flip the paper over to hide the emblem.

"You've been digging through the desk, have you?"

No use lying about it now. Best to get right to the point. She pinned him with a stare. "Are you a guardian?"

His head cocked toward her, but he didn't turn his shoulders her way. "What do you mean?"

"Are you a member of the Guardian of the Bones?"

He pulled to his full height, turning to her and crossing his arms over his chest. "Why would I answer a question like that?"

"Why wouldn't you answer a question like that?" Her glare skewered him. "I can think of only one reason. Are you a guardian?"

"And if I am?"

"Then I would think you are better than this—kidnapping a defenseless woman and holding her captive."

"Then you would think wrong." He glanced down at the paper. "What do you know of the guardians?"

"Enough. Enough to know this"—her arm swung about her—"is not what you do. Unless you're no longer a guardian."

His shoulders lifted and dropped noncommittally. "Once you are a guardian, you are always a guardian."

"Even if you're a lord?"

"You are what you are, no matter what title attaches itself to you. What I am or am not is of no consequence to you or what is happening here in this castle."

More vague statements. The man was going to drive her mad with his ambiguous comments. Which circled her back to the start of this debacle.

She eyed him, her mouth pulling to the side as she tried to quell the rising fury in her voice. "What is it you believe I did? It must be something grievous and you must be wrong about it, for I haven't done a thing to anyone. My only enemy seems to be myself these days."

He stared at her, his countenance not changing a bit. So much so he almost looked like he had fallen asleep with his eyes open.

She took a step closer to him, craning her neck to look up at him. "I don't think you're that good of an actor—this last fortnight, you looked at me with interest, with lust. You kissed me with all of that on your lips."

"Don't flatter yourself."

"Am I? For I know what desire looks like, and I saw it in your eyes. When our bodies brushed against each other while we were dancing. At the way your hand liked to linger over mine when you were passing me drinks. That moment when we were playing tennis and you brushed a lock of hair out of my eyes and then you paused, just staring at me. You wanted me." She moved a last step toward him, collapsing the space between them, her breasts lightly touching his chest. "Do you deny it?"

His jaw ticked. "You have no idea how badly the fire you're playing with will burn you, Georgina."

"Don't I?" She set her hand onto his chest, the hard muscles under his lawn shirt twitching at the touch. "I think the fire I'm playing with is the one that I saw reflected in your eyes when we bumped into each other after I had been swimming at the waterfall and your stare had drifted down to see my dress was wet, my nipples ripe under the fabric. The way your eyes lingered. It was fire. Then you kissed me. And as I walked away, you had to adjust your member. You didn't think I saw it. I did. I saw that fire. Those flames begging to be released."

Wicked quick, he grabbed her neck, forcing her backward until she hit the wall and his mouth slammed down onto her.

Raging and devouring. His tongue pushing inside of her mouth.

His hold on her neck didn't ease, he only shifted his hand up, cupping the back of her jaw so he could angle her head to the side and gain better access to her mouth.

Deeper his tongue plunged, stealing her breath, and his body crushed up against hers, his stiff cock driving into her belly as he wedged his knee in between her legs and pressed up against her folds.

For one wretched second, she reveled in it. Let it take her over. She leaned into his touch, her hips shifting against his knee deep in her crotch.

Too much.

Too much because the fire that lit within her at his touch was the exact opposite of what she'd intended. She'd wanted this reaction in him. Not herself.

The wretched man had kidnapped her and now her folds were pulsating at his touch. Begging for more.

She was wrong in the head. So very wrong.

Abruptly, he yanked his mouth away from her, but his hand stayed clasped about her neck, his fingers thrumming into the soft flesh along her throat as he stared down at her.

Disgust spread across his face.

Disgust at her or at himself, she wasn't sure.

His fingers along her throat tightened, and then he stepped back, yanking his hand away. "Next time you think to play with flames, be prepared to be charred."

He spun and stalked out of the room, slamming the door closed behind him.

Pressed against the wall, she didn't breathe, didn't move for long seconds.

That had been treacherous.

A dangerous game she was playing with him.

Yet something had held him back from taking it any farther.

Hatred? Honor?

Both?

She exhaled a long breath, her mind a whirlwind and her body still ablaze at his touch. At his lips on hers. At his tongue deep into her.

She needed to get out of here. Had to.

Rushing across the room, she looked out the window again, hoping for something she had missed in her early inspection. Light was quickly fading, not that light would have helped her. There was nothing. Nothing but a sheer drop to the ground.

She slumped forward, her hands on the windowsill and her forehead clunking against the glass. For minutes she stayed in place, trying to calm her breathing and the wild energy coursing through her veins.

Then she was left with nothing.

Her limbs went weak, every last drop of energy leaving her.

She hadn't eaten since breaking fast this morning, but the turmoil in her stomach sent her feet toward the bed instead of the food on the desk.

At the bed, she pulled back the coverlet and the sheet, then slipped onto the mattress. Slightly lumpy, it was sunken in on this side. An imprint of Silas's body, like he shared the bed with someone and this half was his.

She scooted toward the middle of the massive bed and ran her hand over the other side of the mattress. Flat.

Whoever he shared it with hadn't been in it for a long time. Or maybe he just liked to hover near an edge when sleeping. Or maybe this wasn't even his room. Maybe she had everything wrong.

Wrong about Silas. Wrong about every thought in his head.

His scent snaked around her.

No, he definitely slept here.

She'd sleep on the floor, but the scent of him would come with the blanket. She looked around the room— nothing else to keep her warm.

Even in summer, a coolness held fast in the stone walls surrounding her.

She let her head fall onto a pillow, too exhausted to fight it anymore, and she pulled the coverlet over her.

Wanting to hate the smell of him, but unable to deny how comforting it was to be wrapped in it.

So she hated herself instead as she drifted into sleep.

{ CHAPTER 14 }

Silas stomped his way into his study and headed straight toward the sideboard holding his immediate salvation.

His head dropping, he stopped in front of the glasses and brandy, his hands clutching onto the edge of the heavy oak sideboard.

What in the bloody hell had he been thinking?

Kissing her.

Kissing her.

Fucking kissing her.

His knuckles bright white, near to popping, he shoved off of the board but didn't take a step back, instead pouring a tumbler full of brandy. So full and haphazard the liquid sloshed over the rim.

A waste, as the 1810 Renault & Co cognac was expensive—the one thing he allowed himself to splurge on—but then a little spilled brandy was the least of his worries at the moment.

Betraying every shred of his being with that kiss was the worry he needed to be concentrating on.

Idiot.

Blasted dung-heap of an idiot, he was.

His tongue greedy for anything other than the taste of Georgina in his mouth, he drank a swallow, holding it on his mouth until his eyes started to water. He swallowed.

Fuck. Still there. Still the taste of her worming into his head, into his being. He tried to spit it out.

Another gulp.

Still there.

He scraped his tongue against his front teeth, willing to draw blood just to rid himself of her.

Another swallow of brandy, another attempt to burn the taste away.

The study door opened and Silas sloshed more brandy into his glass before turning around to the two people walking into the room. Two of the finest guardians around.

He watched Callum and Daphne come into the room. "Did you get something to eat before Cook left?"

Daphne moved to the chair next to the fireplace and turned it toward him, her small form sinking heavy onto the chair as she scrutinized him. "We did. She said she'd be back daily at sunup with food for the day. In and out, like always. She'll be staying at her cousin's farmstead."

Silas nodded. "The rest of the staff is gone as well?"

This wasn't unusual for the staff at Yarstone. The guardians sometimes needed use of the castle without any extra eyes about, so he had sent the staff away numerous times before. They'd be paid, of course, but wouldn't need to come back until Silas sent out word their presence was once more needed.

Callum picked up the iron poker next to the fireplace and prodded at the fire, sending the flames higher and more light into the room. "They are. I got them out and to the stables to leave before you dragged that wench up into your room." He looked up at Silas, the stretch in his neck almost comical for how thick it was. "She secured?"

"For now." Silas took a sip of his drink.

Callum stood straight, hanging the poker next to the fireplace. "How did she get by you?"

"She didn't get by me."

Both Callum's and Daphne's eyebrows lifted at him.

"The little idiot thought to climb out of the window. That was why the glass broke."

Callum scoffed a laugh. "What?"

Silas shook his head, disgust curling his tongue. "She tied strips of a bed sheet together and hung herself out of the damn window."

Daphne nodded, a gleam of appreciation in her mossy green eyes. "She swung over to the battlement?"

"She did."

Callum shook his head. "A rat cornered will do anything to escape."

"That she will." Silas turned around to the sideboard, set his drink down, and poured one each for Callum and Daphne.

He brought them over to them, then retreated to the sideboard, leaning back against it as he picked up his tumbler and took another sip.

"You didn't tell us the full story of what happened at Toften Hall before the glass broke in the tower room." Callum pointed upward. "You said she was involved?"

"She was. As I was saying before the interruption, the chimney sweep verified that one of the Harwall coachmen,

Leroy Wilkins, was the one that shoved Josie under those horses and carriage in London."

"Did you lead the boy?" Daphne asked.

That was Daphne—always a stickler for doing things the proper way.

"No," Silas replied. "I had the boy in the stables and he found the scourge himself."

"The coachman—Wilkins—has been taken care of?"

"He has. By my own hand."

Daphne nodded. "So how is the woman in your room involved? Who is she?"

He'd only managed to tell Daphne and Callum part of the story of Toften Hall before he'd heard the glass break on the tower window and had to run outside and watch Georgina nearly fall to her death.

A shiver ran down his spine at the thought. A shiver he instantly despised.

He took another sip of his drink, looking to Callum and then his stare settled on Daphne. The four of them, Callum, Daphne, Josie and him, had been thick as thieves at one point. "That woman is Georgina Constantine, the niece of the Baron of Harwall and daughter to the previous baron."

Callum gasped a swallow and then started to cough as the liquid choked him. "The Georgina Constantine that Josie was guarding when she was killed?"

"The very same." Silas nodded, his mouth pulling to a tight line.

Daphne's eyes narrowed at him, though she didn't rise from the chair. She always took things on her own time—

that was how a brilliant mind tended to work. "The very same one that you went to Toften Hall to protect? To finish Josie's mission?"

"Yes, her and her sister, Willow."

Daphne's head angled to the side. "Do tell me why that woman is now a captive here at Yarstone."

Silas stilled. Not for effect, more to steel himself against falling into a rage. A rage at the woman currently upstairs in his room. A rage at himself for letting his lips crush onto hers. "She told the coachman to do it."

Callum's glass dropped out of his hand, smashing onto the stone hearth. He jumped back, looking down. "Well, shit." He looked up at Silas. "And shit."

Silas nodded.

"No," Daphne said. "That makes no sense. Josie was there to protect them. She—"

"Georgina was with child," Silas cut her off. "The coachman's child. Josie wouldn't let him near Georgina— had threatened him on numerous occasions, I imagine. Georgina intended to elope with Wilkins. Josie was in the way of that."

"But to kill Josie—"

"The coachman confessed to everything." His stare went pointed at Daphne. "Everything."

Daphne sank back into the cushions of the chair, her look dropping to the glass she held, her forefinger circling the rim of the glass for long seconds. She looked up at Silas. "Then why isn't Miss Constantine dead?"

"Because it's crueler to keep her alive."

"How?"

"She lost the babe. She lost her sister. Truth told, I rather think she was hoping for that rope of sheets to tear away from the tower."

Daphne nodded, her eyes turning into hard glass. "Then let us make this even more difficult for her."

"Exactly what I was thinking." Silas lifted his glass. He knew how close Daphne and Josie had been. Both Daphne and Callum loved Josie just as much as he did.

Callum kicked the broken shards of glass about his boots into the fireplace. "What did you tell Hector? He pulled both of us out of the guardian trainings we were holding to send us here."

Silas shrugged. "I told him I needed you two. It was all he needed to know." Hector wanted to find Josie's killer just as much as the three of them.

Daphne took a sip of her drink, then stood. She handed the glass to Callum and he finished the contents in one massive swallow.

She turned to Silas. "Does Miss Constantine know you are well aware of exactly what she did?"

"No. She's twisting in the wind, not understanding anything that's happening to her right now. I stole her away from Toften Hall, but she doesn't know why. And I want the mystery of it—the injustice of it—to eat away at her and devour her from the inside out. She's a captive here, stolen from everything she knows, but she doesn't have an inkling as to the why. Doesn't have a clue of what I intend to do with her."

"What do you intend?" Daphne took a step toward him. "Frankly, why not just kill her? It's where all this is headed, correct? Why drag Cal and me out here to watch her?"

"Because I need to make an appearance back at Toften Hall so no one suspects I have anything to do with her disappearance."

"Fine." Daphne motioned toward the door. "Introduce us and then you can be on your way."

Silas nodded, then turned toward the door, holding his tongue.

He wasn't about to tell Daphne, of all people, that he needed to get away from the witch before the scene upstairs from earlier repeated itself.

Or that he didn't have it in him to kill Georgina outright.

He'd get to that point. He would. He just had to let the rage fester within him until it had nowhere to go except with a blade straight through Georgina's black heart.

He would get there.

He would.

{ CHAPTER 15 }

"Wake up."

The words filtered into her mind, intruding on the dark sleep she'd slipped into.

Words in and out, easily ignored.

Her arm moved. Not on its own accord. Something nudging it.

"Wake up."

This time the words were harsh, tearing into her consciousness quickly.

Georgina jerked, sitting upright in the bed, her guard instantly up. Sconces had been lit along the wall next to the door, along with the candle beside the bed.

In the shadows, Silas stood next to the bed, a sour look on his face as he stared down at her.

She *was* sleeping in his bed.

And judging by the hatred he'd doused her with in the last six hours, it couldn't be a pleasant sight for him.

She shoved back the coverlet, swinging her feet toward the edge of the bed to get out of it, but he blocked the pathway to get her feet onto the floor.

"Don't bother getting up. I just have one thing I need to do with you." His words laced with menace, the hairs on the back of her neck spiked, but she held his stare. She was beyond gambling with her life at this point, for she had nothing left to lose.

He turned to the side and motioned toward the open doorway.

Georgina followed his gaze out past the doorway of his room and realized a well-lit sitting room was attached to this chamber. Two people appeared in the doorway.

One was a woman with dark hair and green eyes, shorter than Georgina with a petite frame and undeniably pretty.

Juxtaposed next to her was a tall brute of a man, thick, the best way to describe him. Thick arms, thick legs, thick trunk, thick neck. All of it muscle, she easily recognized. For as hard as he looked, he held a spark in his grey eyes that softened him from the scary rank into the moderately unnerving rank.

Blinking the sleep out of her eyes, she looked up at Silas where he still awkwardly blocked her way off the bed.

"This is Daphne and Callum."

Both of them moved several steps into the room.

"Miss Constantine." Callum inclined his head to her, though didn't smile.

Daphne's face twitched, her countenance pulling into a glare.

They both clearly despised her.

How in the hell had that happened? She didn't even know them.

Silas. Silas was why they despised her.

Silas took a step toward them, then looked back at her. "Daphne and Cal are here to be your guards for the time being. You have access to this room, nothing more. They

will feed you when it is necessary. Remove your chamber
pot. Beyond that, don't expect anything out of them."

She swung her feet, still in her boots, down onto the
floor and shoved her skirt into place over her legs. "But…
but that is all? What—"

"Yes, that is all. This room. Daphne or Cal will always
be outside in the sitting room at all times to ensure you
don't attempt an escape. I assume you have already more
thoroughly investigated the nonexistent escape route out the
window?"

She glanced over her shoulder at the window, ire
instantly invading her veins. She'd done nothing—nothing
to deserve any of this—whatever *this* was. For Silas certainly
didn't have any intentions toward her, other than keeping
her captive here.

She looked back at him, fury building in her words.
"Of course, I have."

His top lip twisted, almost like he was holding back a
smile.

Ass.

"And neither will you find a route out past Daphne or
Cal. This room is all you get as it does have the convenience
of the sitting room outside for Daphne and Cal. The room
is a generosity I wasn't originally willing to extend to you."

"So gracious," she spat out.

He folded his arms over his chest. "Would you prefer a
cell in the undercrofts?"

Her mouth clamped shut. She was probably one
unchecked word away from that very fate.

"I thought not." Silas's arms fell to his sides as he turned toward Callum. "Walk me out."

Georgina shot up onto her feet. "Wait. You are leaving?"

He looked back to her. "That is none of your concern."

"But, wait, how long are you to be gone for?"

He didn't answer her, simply turned his back to her and Callum fell in step beside him.

Daphne pulled the door closed behind them, locking it.

Georgina stood beside the bed, still, for several minutes, not comprehending a single thing that was happening around her.

Why kidnap her, then leave her in an old castle?

It made no sense.

Silas wasn't looking to rape her. Wasn't looking to compromise her and force her into marriage. He looked at her with hatred, yet hadn't lifted a finger against her.

She needed to get out of here. Now.

Get out while both Callum and Silas were otherwise occupied.

She'd sized up Daphne. She was taller than the woman, probably stronger. And definitely more desperate. She could get past her.

This was her chance, as long as she acted fast. Darkness was her friend—if she could make it outside of the castle, she could lose herself in the surrounding forest.

Going to her toes on the worn carpet, Georgina crept to the door, trying to not squeak any floorboards. Setting her hand on the back of the door, she pressed her ear to the wood.

Nothing. Not Silas's angry tones or the low rumble of Callum's voice. Not their footsteps.

She waited another several minutes, listening.

Until she couldn't stand it any longer and she tiptoed over to the bed where she blew out the candle and picked up the silver candlestick from the nightstand.

She moved to the side of the door. "Daphne?"

Muttering greeted her and footsteps creaked across the floor, approaching the door. Georgina lifted the candlestick high over her head, poised to strike.

The lock clinked open and the door flung open.

Georgina swung downward with the candlestick and hit…air.

Before she could even catch her balance, her legs were swept out from under her and she fell flat on her face, the candlestick clunking out of her hand and rolling across the floor.

Her face shoved into the carpet, knees dug into her thighs as her left hand was twisted onto her back, then her right.

All of it happening in one instant, before she could even get a breath into her lungs for having the wind knocked out of her in the fall.

She was completely immobilized. Unable to shift on the floor, unable to move either of her arms or her torso. And she tried, squirming, to no avail.

Laughter, vile, drifted down to her. "That was really all you had in you? That took me less than five seconds."

Daphne jammed Georgina's right arm upward along her back, stretching the muscles along her shoulder into pain and a grunt squeaked out of Georgina.

Daphne leaned down, setting her lips next to Georgina's ear, her voice frigid menace. "You don't want to test us, witch."

Georgina could feel it bleeding off of Daphne, the hate dripping down from her.

She couldn't turn her head enough to see Daphne, but she made the effort the best she could as she tried to get air into her lungs. "You hate me just as much as Silas."

"Yes."

"Why?"

Daphne laughed, and the sound of it chilled Georgina to the bone. "You'll get no answers from me."

She released Georgina's right wrist, then her left and viciously dug her knee into the back of Georgina's right thigh as she pushed herself up to stand over Georgina.

Georgina rolled onto her side, looking up at Daphne. "But why? Why will no one tell me a blasted thing?"

The right side of Daphne's face lifted into a smile. A smile that would light up the world if it was complete and lost the air of bleak death. Her glare bored into Georgina. "Because answers are power. And here—here you have no answers."

Georgina shifted, looking out the doorway just as Callum walked into the sitting room. The brute looked at Daphne and then at Georgina on the floor. A brutal smile came to his face, the same hate running through Silas and Daphne reflected in his eyes.

Daphne stepped past her and closed the door.

What in the almighty hell had she done to these people?

{ CHAPTER 16 }

For two weeks Georgina studied them religiously. Studied Daphne's habits. Studied Callum's habits.

Daphne was exacting, precise in every movement she made, every step she took, and she never veered. Never put herself in a vulnerable position when she was delivering food or removing a chamber pot.

And she was fast. Agile. Georgina had experienced that the first night she had met them. The bruises on her cheek from falling flat on her face had only just faded.

Callum, on the other hand, was more easygoing. Not exacting. Not agile, or at least she imagined him to be less agile than Daphne. He probably believed his size and power would get him out of any situation. Which normally would be the case.

But Georgina only needed him to be a bit blunderous—to be a giant oak felling onto the ground for one precious moment—long enough for her to escape out of the room and out of the castle, and into the forest, as had been her original plan.

Callum also had one fatal flaw.

He walked in and out of her room with the key to the door in his right hand, always held loosely, for he was inevitably going to relock the door within seconds.

Neither of them ever stayed in the room. They never talked to her, no matter how she tried to engage them. They delivered a tray of food, took the dirty one and left the

room. The same with the chamber pot. Clean one in. Dirty one out.

That was the extent of their interaction with her.

Stone walls, the both of them, down to their dusty, impenetrable exteriors.

At least with her.

The longest moment either one had stared at her—and it had been Callum—was when she'd started to wear Silas's clothes after five days of being in her same shift and dress. His lawn shirt swam about her limbs, but she'd rolled up the sleeves and she'd set a waistcoat to hang loosely from her shoulders, mostly for modesty as the white shirt let a little too much light through to her nipples. She'd had to fold up the bottom of his trousers and used braces to hold them on her body.

Not the most charming guise, but it sufficed well enough for sitting around the room all day and night.

Outside her door, she could often hear Callum and Daphne talking, laughing. Playing cards or hazard. She'd seen glimpses of the books they had stacked in the sitting room—all sorts of entertainment to pass the time. While she just had the paper in the desk and some ink to entertain herself. That was the extent of it, and the whole of the unending minutes ticking by was driving her quite mad.

Georgina had initially thought she could get one of them to thaw to her—probably Callum—but no amount of cajoling or sweet requests or tears or smiles could break either of them.

While Daphne's quick disposal of her echoed the same movements Miss Sanders had used with aggressive gentlemen when she had been protecting them, Georgina had her suspicions as to whether or not Silas and Callum and Daphne were actually part of the Guardians of the Bones.

The guardians were honorable people—Miss Sanders had possessed a bottomless well of honor and valor and intelligence within her.

Not these people.

All of them were the exact opposite of Miss Sanders. Cold and callous and not caring for an innocent woman caught in someone's scheme.

It had taken her days to realize no shining knight was going to ride in and save her.

She had to be her own knight.

If she was going to save herself, that meant one thing. She had to get out of here before Silas returned. Tonight was that night.

She'd changed back into her shift and dress, as she was determined to make it happen.

Callum was on duty in the sitting room, and she had heard Daphne come in with the trays of food, then her footsteps receded out into the hallway.

Callum always ate first.

She knew because her food was always cold and she could smell whatever he'd eaten on his person before he set the tray down.

True to form, a half hour after Daphne had delivered the trays to the room, Callum set the key into the lock.

Georgina was ready, crouched alongside the doorframe.

The door swung open and Callum moved in, the latest tray of food balanced in his left hand, the key in his right.

Georgina yanked up on the rope she'd twisted out of strips of one of Silas's lawn shirts and had strung across the doorway at shin height.

Callum stepped directly into it and he tripped, falling forward like a giant oak tree.

She dropped the rope at the same time she reached up and ripped the key from his hand. By the time he landed flat on the floor, she had sprung up, dragging the door closed.

He scrambled, reaching for the door just as it slammed closed. Her hand shaking, the key went in the lock, turning, and he was locked in.

A roar vibrated the floorboards under her feet, but miraculously, it wasn't loud on this side of the door. The stone walls and heavy ancient wood worked wonders to muffle the sound.

The pounding started—enough to shake the door on its hinges and Georgina spun, running to the doorway of the sitting room, and then peeked out into the hallway. She wasn't about to stick around to see how long it would take for him to tear that door down, or for Daphne to finally hear him.

Little by little, she made her way through the castle, running, peeking around corners, then sprinting her way downward through the maze of corridors and turns until she finally found a door that led outside.

Darkness had just set upon the land and without
another thought, she sprinted as fast as she could into the
cover of the forest.

Her hands ripping against bark with branches tearing
at her, she dodged trees and forced her legs to keep moving,
only one thought pulsating in her mind.

Run.

{ CHAPTER 17 }

A light.

One of the few in this small village.

Georgina didn't know how long it had been since she'd escaped from the castle. Two hours? Three? Four?

Her legs had started to fail long ago, but she forced them to keep moving, to keep working until she was out of the forest and somewhere—anywhere—but in that cage of a room again.

She'd eventually stumbled upon a road and had followed it—not on it, but adjacent to it, a few steps inside the treeline, just in case Daphne or Callum came barreling down it on horses, ready to grab her.

The road had led her to this.

A small village nestled in a little valley, with only one crossroad in the middle of the town.

The road that split the town in two seemed empty, almost all of the shops and the houses dark—as would be usual at this time of night in the country. This wasn't London where everything started to sparkle alive once the sun disappeared from the sky.

But there—a light in a window.

She crept up to the window and peeked inside.

Salvation, she hoped.

A wide-open room sat beyond the window with several round tables in it, all of them empty. Not quite a tavern or a coaching inn, it had to be a boarding house.

Looking over her shoulder to make sure no one had come along the road, she shuffled toward the main door and lifted the knocker. Letting it drop, she repeated the action three times, then quickly ran her hands over her hair, trying to shove all the loose strands into her haphazard chignon.

Thank goodness she hadn't let her hair descend into a complete rat's nest during the last fortnight. She'd only had her fingers to comb her hair, but she'd also had hours upon hours to work her way through it.

An older woman in a dull grey dress that lifted her bosom high out in front of her opened the door with a smile on her face. A smile that disappeared the moment she spotted Georgina.

Her brow wrinkled as she looked Georgina up and down. "My, my, what have we here? Ye are not from our town. Are ye lost?"

Georgina nodded. "You guess correctly. I am. I got separated from my traveling companions and stumbled upon your village. It seems as though my directions got mixed up." She stepped toward the woman, trying to shuffle her backward so she could land herself in the safety of the foyer and close the door behind her. "Is this a boarding house?"

The woman's right eyebrow lifted. "Ye aren't a swindler are ye? We don't take beggars here."

Georgina motioned to her dress. "Do my clothes look like I am a beggar?" She knew the rich turquoise muslin dress fit her body well, even if she'd lost a quarter stone during the past fortnight of only eating porridge and stew, with a few meat pies sprinkled in.

"Well, child, no, ye don't look like a beggar, but I've been fooled before." The older woman leaned against the doorframe, her arms clasped under her hefty bosom.

"I can assure you, I am not a beggar. And my uncle will be very happy to pay you well for your kindness in housing me here tonight, if you will."

"Yer uncle?" Her eyebrows lifted with sudden interest. "Who is he?"

"He is Lord Harwall."

"Oh? Never heard of him. But fancy, eh? We don't get fancy coming through here very often." Her right fingers tapped along her left elbow, her interest waning.

"I promise you, ma'am, I will make certain he pays you well for your kindness."

She stared at Georgina for a long moment, then let out a long sigh. "Fine. Ye look a mite tired. And ye look like ye could use a bath. I just had one brought up into my room, but ye can use both the bath and my bed tonight."

That, Georgina wasn't expecting. "What? No—I couldn't displace you. Any old bed is fine."

"No, if ye are going to be a recipient of my kindness, then ye get the whole of it." The woman unwrapped her arms and reached out for Georgina, taking her elbow. "Let's get ye into the bath and I'll see what is left in the kitchens from tonight."

Georgina nodded as the door closed behind her, tears brimming in her eyes at the first crumb of kindness she had seen in weeks. "Thank you, so very much, miss…"

"Mrs. Collier. Though I am a widow, done ten years now." She guided Georgina up the wide staircase off the foyer.

"Thank you, Mrs. Collier." Her legs weak, they started to cramp to where she could barely move them, but she forced one leg up the stairs, then the next, trying to not lean on Mrs. Collier too much. "You don't know what this means to me."

"A lot, child. I can see it in yer eyes." She patted Georgina's hand. "What is your name?"

"Georgina."

"Well, we will get ye right before we get ye on yer way tomorrow. Where is it ye were headed to?"

"To Buckinghamshire. Toften Hall to be specific." Except no. The house party would have long ago disbanded. She gave the older woman a tight smile. "Then onward to London."

Mrs. Collier nodded. "We have a man in town that makes the route to London every Tuesday and Friday, and I believe he may go along through Buckinghamshire on his way to London. I'll have to ask him, though. It is just a wagon with goods he has, but he can bring ye there tomorrow or at least close to where ye need to go if you would like?"

"I would. Thank you for that."

The bath was merely a hip bath with barely heated water, but it was the most glorious bath Georgina had ever had. Enough to get the oils off her body, scrub her hair, and wipe away all the thin scabs the branches had torn at her arms and hands on her way through the forest.

She was drying off with a threadbare towel when
Mrs. Collier reappeared with some bread and marmalade.
Georgina paused, draping the towel in front of her body
and tucking it about her backside.

"'Tis not much, but it will fill yer belly for the night so
ye can sleep well." Mrs. Collier set the plate down on the
top of a low chest and went to a dresser, pulling out a shift.

She shook out the folds and held the shift out to
Georgina to measure it up. "It will be big on ye, as I am
more fleshy up top than ye, but it is clean." She laid it atop
the simple wooden chair by the fireplace. "We can even
stitch it in a bit in the morning so it will fit under that dress
of yours."

Tears started to brim in Georgina's eyes, the woman's
kindness overwhelming her. "Again, I thank you, Mrs.
Collier. Your kindness is appreciated."

"'Tis luck that brought ye to my door, and I am not one
to scorn luck." Mrs. Collier stoked the coals in the fireplace
and then picked up her candlestick, moving toward the
door. "Sleep well. I will awaken ye well before it is time to
meet the wagon."

"Thank you."

Mrs. Collier left the room and Georgina finished
drying off, then slipped into the simple shift. Slightly
scratchy, but it would do.

She ate a few bites of the bread, but soon enough, her
stomach told her it was in no mood for food and began to
flip. She probably wouldn't be ready to eat for real until she
was safe at home in London.

Georgina set the bread down, took a sip of the slightly bitter wine Mrs. Collier had set down, and crawled into the bed, relief finally flowing through her legs.

By tomorrow, she would be back in London. Safe in her own bed.

She just had to suffer a few hours more.

{ CHAPTER 18 }

The door opening woke Georgina up, and she blinked in the darkness.

For an instant, she thought she was still at Yarstone until the thin sheet scratched along her arm and the distinct lack of Silas's scent told her she had finally gotten out of the castle.

The village. Mrs. Collier.

She looked to the window and the partially pulled drapes.

It couldn't already be time to leave for London—her body felt like it had just fallen asleep.

Moonlight still streamed in the window, but the coals in the fireplace had long since died down, only a few glowing embers still lending light to the room.

She groaned to herself.

Too early, but then, the man travelling to London probably wanted to be out of town before the break of day.

She shifted, turning over in the bed toward the doorway as the door clicked closed. The form in the dark shadows turned to her and her half-drawn eyes opened wide.

That didn't look like Mrs. Collier.

Boots clomped across the floor and arms were moving. A jacket coming off. A flash of a white shirt. Buttons on trousers.

A *man* in her room.

Mrs. Collier's room. Whoever this was must think she was Mrs. Collier.

She sat up in the bed, holding the blanket close to her chest.

"Excuse me, sir, I think you have the wrong room. Mrs. Collier is sleeping elsewhere tonight."

"Don't think so, kitty. Mae promised me a new one tonight and ye are it."

The fall front of his trousers fell open and his erection, glowing white and large in the scant moonlight filled her eyes.

"No. No." She scooted back on the bed, fear starting to wrap around her belly. "You are mistaken. I am not here for your pleasure. I am just here for the night, nothing more."

"No, I paid for ye fair and square. Mae don't make mistakes."

"Paid?" Hell. She was in a whorehouse. Not a boarding house.

Georgina scrambled off the bed, putting the bed between her and the man. The only problem being that both of those things were between her and the door.

Her right hand held the blanket to her chest as she lifted her left hand to reason with him. "Truly, this is a mistake. Mrs. Collier took me in for the night and I will be leaving in a few hours. I'm not a whore. I was just lost. I am sure there are plenty of ladies here that will attend to your needs."

"Not like ye will, kitty. I've had them all and I paid extra for new meat. Ye're it."

"No." She dropped the blanket and darted out past the bed, running for the door.

The second her fingers touched the doorknob, he caught her around the waist and flung her back into the room.

She tried to barrel forward, going for the door again and he smacked her across the face, sending her sprawling to the floor. "Mae said ye'd be feisty, just like I like it."

Dazed, her head not right, she tried to look up but only saw sparking dots around three fireplaces vying for position in front of her.

Before she could even recognize he was on top of her, he grabbed her wrist and twisted her up off the floor, then shoved her onto the bed.

"No. Stop. Stop. Please stop." She swung her fists in a fury. She connected with flesh, once, twice, and he grabbed both of her wrists, yanking them above her head and pinning her to the bed.

Terror, guttural and ripping her to shreds, invaded her body, and she twisted, kicking, still trying to fight him off. Screaming. Every second that passed, her power slipping away.

Away.

"Keep screaming, little kitty. That's the way. Keep screaming." His head dove down to her, his tongue coming out and licking her neck up onto her face and the line he'd cut across her cheek.

"The blood. So good. Mae's going to get extra coin for this."

He twisted her into place, her screams, her fight useless against him.

Like she was nothing.

Insignificant against the man pressing down on her. His knee wedging her shift upward between her legs, forcing her into position.

Every bit of her resistance bled out onto the bed, useless, until the fight started to leave her.

Until she knew she had no power against this.

Only horrified acceptance that it was going to happen and there was nothing she could do to stop it.

Nothing.

{ CHAPTER 19 }

His stomach dropped to his toes.

Screaming, crying, her legs kicking, Georgina struggled against the wretched cur forcing her onto the bed, his knee, his hands yanking up her shift.

Then her fight suddenly ceased, and she stilled like her spirit left her body.

Deranged rage bloodied the world around him and Silas charged forward, grabbing the half-dressed man by the back of his neck, and he ripped him off of Georgina. He threw him across the room, straight into the fireplace, and the man's instant screams told him that the burning coals were doing their job.

Barbaric. But the man deserved barbaric. He was touching Georgina. Forcing himself on her.

Barbaric was a mercy for how he wanted to tear the arms off the scum.

He veered to the bed to scoop Georgina up in his arms, not willing to waste the time it would take to beat the man into a mangled mess when he needed to get her out of this place.

His teeth bit his tongue at the fact that she was only wearing a thin shift. That blood was smeared across her face from a cut on her lip.

She didn't fight him, didn't try to scramble off the bed away from him. Like he was the lessor evil. Which wasn't something she would believe.

No, she didn't fight because her eyes were glazed over like she wasn't even present.

A small favor.

Curling her into his chest, with one arm under her back and the other under her legs, he carried her down the stairs, shoving past Mrs. Collier standing at the bottom of the steps, watching him with interest.

His rage found a target. "Truly, Mae? This is what I find? Truly?"

Pulling her shawl tighter across her shoulders and wrapping it in front of her ample cleavage, Mae lifted her shoulders. "I didn't know she was yers, mi'lord."

Yours?

An arrow of a word, it split into his chest. A spiky bur that wedged into his lungs, making it hard to breathe.

Georgina wasn't his. That was the last thing she was.

Yet he was carrying her out of Mae's whorehouse like she was precious China.

He sliced Mae in two with his glare. "Doesn't matter who she is, you shouldn't enable that scene that I walked into upstairs to anyone."

"How was I supposed to know she wasn't a whore?" Mrs. Collier scurried in front of him to open the door. "She came in alone, hungry and needing help. That's how all my girls come in. Tonight wasn't different at all."

"Not everyone knows this is a whorehouse."

She scoffed a laugh. "Everyone within twenty miles knows it. Those are the only folk that matter."

Silas charged out the door and into the night air, making sure to hit Mrs. Collier's shoulder with Georgina's bare feet as he pushed past her.

He couldn't kick the woman, but he sure as hell could have Georgina do it for him.

Straight to his horse, he lifted Georgina and set her on his saddle, her legs dangling off the side. He kept one hand on her lap as he didn't trust her to not just fall off the opposite side of the horse, then he grabbed the reins and vaulted up, seating himself behind her, his arms wrapped around her. A tight fit on the saddle, but it would do.

Out of the village in a minute, he stared down at her head. Her hair was loose about her shoulders, still slightly damp from an earlier bath. He could only partly see her face, but her eyes still looked glazed, disorientated.

"How did you find me?" Her words came slow, like she was just waking up.

"I arrived at Yarstone hours ago and found out you had escaped. Cal and Daphne are still combing the countryside, looking for you."

Her hand lifted, weak, to point back at the village, then fell into her lap. "Did you set that up—set that up with that man? Have him attack me?"

"What? Hell, Georgina, what kind of a monster do you think I am?"

Silence.

Only silence as a response.

He probably deserved that.

As it turned out, during these last weeks he learned he was capable of more savagery than he'd ever thought possible. A monster had always been lurking within him.

Still, her silence felt like a knife stabbing into his gut and twisting.

He let loose a sigh. "No. No, I did not set that up with Mae or with anyone. How would I even know that you escaped?"

"You knew when I tried to get out of the tower."

"You broke the window. It was fairly obvious."

She nodded. More to herself than to him, and her head curled downward, hiding almost all of herself from him. Was she about to lose consciousness?

He shifted both of the reins into his right hand and set the top knuckle of his left forefinger under her chin, lifting her face to him.

Moonlight hit her haunting eyes, the blue in them darker than usual, like the weight of the last two weeks had seeped into her soul, the torment of it darkening everything about her, including her spirit. She was still dazed. Her eyes seeing, but not seeing.

He studied her face in the scant light. At the way the moonlight curled across her cheekbones, setting strands of her loose hair to a golden glow. At the slight furrow in her brow, as though she was trying desperately but unsuccessfully to figure everything out around her. At her lips.

Damn, her lips.

The right side of them puffy from being struck, the splatter of blood smeared out along the outer edge of her lips.

His thumb lifted, wiping the blood away.

She didn't like blood. Especially her own blood. And damned if he didn't want her to see it. He didn't want—

Stop.

What in the hell?

He yanked his hand away from her face. Nagging, ruthless regret swift to swallow him whole.

He needed to snap out of it. Snap out of whatever witchery she'd just set upon him to make him do that.

Enemy.

She was the enemy.

The one that had killed Josie. Killed her.

He had merely reacted at the whorehouse as he would walking into that scene with any woman. No one deserved what that man was about to do to Georgina. That was what this was.

Pity.

Nothing more.

His arms tensed around her and her head fell down into its bowed position, though her body stayed upright and stiff. As though she was trying to hold herself as still as the jostling steps of the horse allowed.

She wasn't about to let him touch her any more than necessary, even if his arms had to be wrapped around her.

She didn't want to touch him.

He didn't want to touch her.

It didn't matter, for the one part of her body that would do the most amount of damage in this position—the side of her hip—was firmly entrenched against his crotch. Every sway of the horse sending her to rub against his cock.

His traitorous Judas of a cock that already had plans that were the exact opposite of what he intended to do to her.

He ignored the vexing pulsating in his rock-hard shaft. Back to the castle. Lock her up.

The rest of the ride went by in insufferable silence.

They reached the castle just as dawn was breaking, and he alighted. He tied the reins to the post and looked up at her sitting on the saddle. In the orangey glow of the sunrise filtering in through the surrounding forest, she looked like a magical wood nymph. Nothing but a white shift on, her hair looking more red than blond as the warm light hit it. The strands of her hair loose and long and wild about her head and hanging down near to her elbows.

No wonder all the men at Toften Hall would turn their heads whenever she walked into a room or stepped onto a dance floor. They saw this ethereal glow about her. Hell, he saw it in her. Saw it in her time and again. Had been entranced by it.

Stop. Stop. Stop.

The fortnight away from Yarstone was supposed to have cured him of looking at her like this.

He set his mouth into a hard line. "Walking or carrying?"

Her chin lifted ever so slightly. "Walk."

She knew exactly where she had to go, and he had to admit he had a speck of respect for the pride in her voice.

He grabbed her about the waist and lifted her from the horse, then set her on the gravel of the drive.

The sharp rocks had to be digging into her bare feet, but she didn't so much as flinch.

Damn. More blood was smeared across her cheek than he had thought. His hand lifted to wipe it away, but then he caught himself.

He hated seeing the blood on her, but he hated himself more for hating the blood on her.

It's what he should want—need. Her blood.

But it only brought a sour taste to his tongue.

She started across the short distance to the door, her steps careful and slow, trying to not let the rocks dig too hard into the soles of her feet.

He didn't reach out to help steady her.

He had to remember what she was.

A killer.

She made it to the wide front step and she shuffled her feet along the front edge of the stone, flicking free tiny stones that had stuck to her soles.

He opened the door and motioned her inward.

She stepped in past him and he closed the door. "Be grateful it was me that found you. Had it been Cal, I think he would have torn you in two. He probably still will when he sees you."

A deep-set frown curved her lips. "I did not injure him, did I?"

"What do you care?"

"He's here on your orders. He hates me just the same as you, but I do not fault him or Daphne for my captivity."

Silas nodded. "You injured his pride, and with him, that was enough for his everlasting ire."

He set his hand on her lower back, ushering her up the central staircase of the castle to the floor of his chambers. Through the sitting room and into his bedroom, and her shoulders dropped considerably as she looked around.

The broken plate and food were still splattered all over the floor. Callum had told him how she had escaped, and Silas had to admit, it had been a clever move on her part.

"Thank you." She looked back at him.

His brows drew together. For what? For locking her up again? He glared at her. "Why?"

"You stopped what was happening to me in that bedroom. In that...whorehouse." Her hands clasped together in front of her belly. "I know you hate me. I know you didn't need to help. I know you probably wanted just as much to stand and watch what was about to happen with a smile on your face. But you didn't. Thank you for that."

"You think I'd watch that with a smile on my face?" His ire instantly spiked. "You don't know the first thing about me."

Her right eyebrow lifted. "That much is glaringly obvious."

She went over to the chest of drawers and pulled out a linen cloth, unfolded it, then dropped to her knees on the floor and began to collect the shards of the plate and the meat pie that had splattered everywhere.

He watched her, watched the thin shift she wore stretched against her backside, the cloth near to transparent with the morning light streaming in through the window.

His hand reached down, adjusting his still hard cock.

Everything about her in that moment willing him to break. To ignore everything he knew of her.

Dammit. He never should have come back to Yarstone so early.

But if he hadn't...

She would be crumpled into a mess at Mae's at this moment, a shell of who she'd been.

The devil take it. How could she have been so stupid to put herself in that situation in the first place?

He couldn't slam his cock into her, so he did the only thing he could with the anger coursing through him. Yell at her.

"Why in the almighty hell did you go there—straight to a whorehouse?"

Her hands paused, a sloppy pea in her fingers and she looked up over her shoulder at him. "I didn't know what that place was. I thought it was a boardinghouse."

He folded his arms across his chest. "And you couldn't figure out what Mae was? One look at her and you should have known. It was idiotic on your part—how can you be so debauched and so naïve at the same time?"

Her face crumpled at his words. They hit exactly as intended and she looked away from him, her stare out the window. "I'm naïve because we've never been anywhere—we stayed at my family's estate in Essex all my life." She sat back onto her calves, her hands falling heavy into her lap,

her fingers still clutching that sole pea that she stared down at. "I've never really been anywhere but in ballrooms and estates. Never out enough to recognize a whorehouse from a boardinghouse."

She shook her head, still staring at the pea. "What do you want from me?"

"How about the smallest sliver of smarts? How about fighting what was happening to you in that whorehouse?"

Her look snapped up to him. "I did fight it."

"Not hard enough."

Her hands flew up at her sides. "It didn't work—so what was I supposed to do?"

"Didn't anyone teach you anything?"

"Like what?"

He stepped toward her, his hands falling to his sides. "Like if a man has his prick out and is about to force himself on you, your first option is to knee or hit him in his ballocks. The pain of it won't stop him from beating you, but it will stop him from raping you, at least for a while. Didn't your family teach you anything of value?"

Her head snapped backward and blazes lit in her eyes. "I know French. That seems valuable. I know how to sew. I know how to manage a household. Account for finances." She stood up, throwing the pea down onto the mess of the spilled food and facing him fully. "A little Italian. My Latin is passable. I know about politics and all the latest proposals floating about parliament. I know about horse racing and how to dance to any music that is played. I know how to interpret Shakespeare and Voltaire. I know about animal husbandry. I know how to cross-pollinate strains of roses.

But no. No, they never did teach me how save myself from a man attacking me."

"Then they undereducated you."

Her head fell back, her eyes to the ceiling. When her chin dropped, her glare carved into him. "I imagine you are accustomed to women that know how to handle themselves, like Daphne, but I am not one of those." Her eyes closed, her chest lifting in a heavy sigh that sent her nipples dark against the shift. "I don't truly know what I'm doing most of the time."

His right eyebrow quirked. "Which means?"

"It means I am the big sister and I was supposed to be protecting Willow from everything and I didn't know what I was doing. I haven't since the day we left Essex and moved to London for the season. I don't know what the hell I'm doing and that fact was pounded with brutality into my skull months ago."

Silas stilled. "What happened months ago?"

"Nothing." She waved her hand in the air and turned, starting to kneel once more to continue cleaning up the mess. "Forget I said anything. Forget I even spoke."

He caught her arm before her knees touched the ground, yanking her upright and turning her toward him. "What happened months ago?"

She shook his hold off her arm and stepped back, her look going toward the open doorway. "What happened at that whorehouse—that was nothing. Nothing compared to what I saw in London, nothing compared to how life can turn."

"What happened to you in London?"

Her shoulders lifted high. "Everything in my world fell apart and I couldn't stop it—no matter how I wanted it to be different, I couldn't will it into being." Her voice wavered. "I found out I am insignificant. I am nothing."

His eyes narrowed. "What happened?"

She looked up at the ceiling, shaking her head. "Death came. Death right in front of me, and I couldn't stop it." Her gaze dropped to him. "I know about the Guardians of the Bones because we had hired one, her name was Miss Sanders, though I do not know if that was her real name. Did you know her?"

His lips pursed, his stare locked on her.

"No. No, I don't suppose you would tell me if you did. Even if you are a guardian."

He blinked, his stare unmoving. "What happened?"

Her mouth opened, words at the tip of her tongue, then her mouth clamped closed, her head bobbing as her eyes squeezed shut. "No. I cannot. I do not think of that day. Ever."

"Do it now." A command, not an ask.

Her eyes crept open to him, and she stared at him for a long moment, then took a trembling breath.

"Miss Sanders was our guardian, she protected Willow and me. And she also became my dear friend and I loved her. Loved her for all she did for us. For her wit and her laughter and her kindness. She could snap a man's bones in two, but she also had this incredibly soft side to her in how she took care of me and Willow. But then she died. She died right in front of me. Died holding my hand. I watched the life leave her eyes and I had never seen anyone die before and I kept thinking if I just held her hand and told her again and again to hold on—to live—she would. Because isn't that how life works? If you want something badly enough, it will happen? Except it didn't. She didn't. My friend left this world crumpled and in agony in front of me and I couldn't do anything to stop the horror of it."

She hiccupped a gasp, her fingers moving in front of her lips as she tried to steady the burgeoning tears.

He had to force his words to remain even. "Her death affected you?"

"It didn't just affect me, it ruined me. Ruined my soul." Her fingers dropped away from her face. "How she died— there was so much pain in her eyes. She was so young, my same age, but she was so much the better person than I. She knew everything about life—how to navigate London, how to fight, how to move about society, she knew it all." She chuckled. "She would have been very good at kneeing a man in the ballocks."

She paused, and her eyes closed as she exhaled a long breath. "And I knew nothing. I just bumbled along, pretending I knew what I was doing in London because I was the older sister—I was supposed to be the guide, the one to protect Willow—when I knew nothing. And then Miss Sanders died. She was such a good person. A rare soul that belonged on this earth for the good she did."

Georgina turned away from him as the tears sprung fully into her eyes, overflowing onto her cheeks and her arms wrapped around her middle. "I watched it all leave her. Her spark, her life. It gutted me. It lifted the veil on

what is real and not in this world. That death was so easy, it would always be ready to take someone I loved."

Silas could see in the way her body trembled, how deeply she felt the loss of Josie. The smallest seed of dread started to sprout deep in his belly.

She coughed out a laugh, raw and caustic. "The worst of it was that it was my fault."

"Your fault?" A spike of anger shot along his spine.

Her forefinger and thumb reached up, rubbing her eyes. "It was just days after she'd taken me to meet with a midwife and I found out I was with child. I was so stupid—I told Leroy about the babe and he questioned it. Questioned if the child was his—he damn well questioned it. Claimed it wasn't his when he was the only one…" Her head shook, her voice spiking in anger.

"And that sent me plunging into a dark place…a very dark place. But Miss Sanders was there for me when I couldn't tell anyone. She walked around London with me for hours, day after day, while I was in a stupor, because I didn't know what to do. She just knew she couldn't bring me home every day until it was late at night and everyone else was already retired or gone for the evening. She was out that day because of me. Out on that sidewalk waiting for me. We were supposed to be at a planning tea for a charity ball that afternoon, but she made excuses for me so I didn't have to be around people. She was there, in front of that carriage, in front of those horses because of me."

Her shoulders hunched over as a sob overtook her, but then she shook her head, blowing out a tortured breath of air. "Then she died in front of me. Died with her fingertips digging into my palm. Mud splatters on her beautiful face. Her lips opening and closing like she needed to tell me all the wisdom of the world before she went. And I haven't been right since."

Silas stared at the side of her face, at the torment that racked her thin slip of a body in that transparent shift. For all that Georgina had set into motion, watching her sins manifest in front of her had obviously been jarring and sympathy started to bleed from the smallest part of him.

He cleared his throat, his heart thundering in his chest. He wanted to be immune to her—*needed* to be immune. Still, words came. "How have you not been right?"

"Well, there was the babe, most of all." Her chest lifted in a heavy sigh as she attempted to overcome the tears and she looked to him. "And because of that I have been stupid, not able to navigate anything, or to think clearly at any turn. And with that, I failed Willow. She was the one thing I had managed to do right in my life up until London— protect her—and then I failed. Miserably and utterly failed. I was too consumed with trying to make sure everything appeared perfect in our lives, that everything was fine, that I managed to forget that things were decidedly not fine. The threats from Lord Fugal were worse than ever upon my life, upon Willow's life after Miss Sanders died. But I tried to pretend they weren't as bad as they were. I failed Willow and now she's gone and I cannot help her."

"No, you cannot. Whatever has happened to Willow has already happened. You cannot change it."

She turned fully toward him and took a step forward. "Please, just let me go, Silas. I need to find my sister. I

cannot change what has happened, but I can still be there for her."

He shook his head. "It is not going to happen. You don't deserve it."

Her lip snarled, her words bitter. "You ass. You asked for this—demanded—a part of me and I gave it to you. Willingly. And then you callously throw it back in my face because you are the devil. You are all the worst of huma—"

He stepped forward and grabbed the back of her head and crashed his lips into her.

Sudden emotion surging so violently within him that it didn't have anywhere to go but to descend down upon her. Kissing her. Marking her as he wanted to do since the moment he found her at the brothel.

Lewd and brutal and rough and she froze for a second.

Froze, but then her arms wrapped around his neck, pulling him into her.

With that one motion, his rock-hard resistance against her snapped deep within him.

He'd wanted this since he first met her—to kiss her for real, with abandon. Raw. Tasting her. Finding the soul of her.

Her lips opened fully to him, kissing him back, giving him full access and he plunged his tongue into her.

A carnal mewl vibrated in the back of her throat.

The sound spurring him for more of the same, he backed her up, pushing her onto the bed, following her down, his lips devouring her and then dropping onto her neck, onto her chest.

The fabric of her chemise loose, he tugged it down, exposing her right nipple, and he clasped it in his mouth, his tongue swirling around the bud. It only took seconds for it to harden, peaked for him, and he moved to her left breast while his mind stormed with manic thoughts.

For all that he hated her. Hated what she had done. He still wanted to twist her angst into something that felt good. He wanted her screaming from his tongue on her. Wanted her bucking under his touch.

Wanted that more than he hated her in the moment.

Hell, he wanted it because he hated her. Hated what her body did to him. Hated how her eyes looked at him, wounded and betrayed. Hated how nothing but spite spewed from her mouth when the only thing that should be in her mouth was his cock.

Her breath panting, her hands threaded into his hair, pulling, prodding him onward. So he went lower, tugging the shift downward. Off her arms. Past her belly.

His lips trailing after the cloth.

Lower.

Past her waist and she didn't stop him, didn't make any motion to deny him or utter words of resistance.

For as much as she hated him, she wanted this just as much.

He dragged the cloth down her legs and dropped it to the floor as he shifted his hands inward. His fingers moved in along her slit, finding her drenched with need.

Her back arched at the touch, her eyes closed as her fingers tightened in his hair. He could feel the pounding waves of blood in her veins at each swipe of his fingers.

Dropping onto his knees, he pushed her legs apart, then lifted her hips, dragging her to the edge of the bed. In the next breath, he dove inward, his tongue passing her slit to drag along her folds.

Her body jerked, coming off the bed, a high-pitched groan at her lips. He sank deeper into her, his tongue working her folds, finding her nub, already peaked and straining for him.

Circling her nub, he slipped one finger into her, then two. Sliding in and out, searching for the spot along her inner walls that would twist her body, making her his.

He knew when he hit it, for her body started to writhe, squirming, so he grazed the spot again and again with his fingers.

He sped his tongue, circling, drawing a hard line with it over and over as he pumped his fingers in and out of her.

The screams weren't a surprise when they came. She was fire. A dragon.

They came, one after another, louder and louder with each stroke until her heels were digging into his back, her body curled over and her words begging with every breath.

Too fast.

He slowed, making her agonize as he yanked her away from the pinnacle before devouring her and pushing her up to that fine line again. He repeated it more times than he could count. His own muscles straining, he manipulated her body until her words didn't make sense, until the only thing in her world was him and what he was making her feel.

And then he needed it—probably more than her. His lips clamped around her nubbin, his tongue working it as he sent three fingers deep into her, hitting that inner spot and not letting it go.

Her screams as she came were the most glorious sound he'd ever heard.

Her body quivered around him, every clench of her muscles vibrating onto his hands, into his mouth.

Her screams of pleasure only made him want more. He wanted to drive his cock into her, imprint himself so hard on her that she came again and again under his thrusts.

Her gasps continued, searching for breath as she came down from the height of the orgasm and it twisted the thought of pleasure in his mind.

Twisted pleasure into pain.

Pain.

Josie's pain.

Josie's pain as she died.

What the hell was he doing?

A few tears and he was fooled?

Just because Georgina hated to see Josie die, it didn't mean that she hadn't asked for his wife's death. People want a nice platter of beef, but they don't want to witness the cow dying, being drained of blood.

Death was so much neater when it was done out of view. Out of thought.

Disgust overwhelmed him at his own actions and he shoved himself off of her legs, stumbling onto his feet, the back of his hand dragging across his mouth, wiping her juices off his lips.

Out.

Away from the demon of this woman.

She pushed herself up on the bed, her head shaking, her eyes distraught through the haze of her pleasure. "What—what happened? What did I do?"

He didn't say a thing.

Couldn't say a thing.

He could only stalk out of the room, slamming the door closed behind him.

{ CHAPTER 20 }

Silas walked into the room, holding a platter of bread and marmalade on his arm. He glanced down toward the floor the minute the door swung open. He wasn't about to fall for Callum's folly.

No tripping line. No escape plan waiting to be hatched.

A twinge of disappointment flickered in his chest. Georgina's tenacity in escaping was admirable, and a small part of him was curious what she would try next.

Georgina was fast asleep in the chair by the fireplace, her neck awkwardly angled as though she'd fallen asleep sitting there, not planning ahead to make herself comfortable. She had put on one of his lawn shirts—he squinted at her legs folded half under her—and a pair of his trousers. She had ripped the bottom half off of each leg, so the ragged edges hit her shins.

A pang of guilt cut across his gut.

He shouldn't have touched her. Much less kissed her. Much less had her writhing under his mouth and hands.

His cock twitched at the vision of her coming dancing through his mind. He shouldn't have done it, but he'd damn well enjoyed it. Even if he'd hated himself afterward.

He lightened his steps so he wouldn't wake her as he went to the desk to set the platter down. He glanced out the window. The morning light had given way to grey skies that threatened rain, but appeared to be holding steady against letting loose the smallest drop.

What had she been doing in his room by herself this last fortnight, save for tearing apart his wardrobe?

He turned around, looking about the room. Nothing much out of place. The mess on the floor from earlier now collected and wrapped in the cloth sitting by the door. His gaze ran over Georgina, and his look paused at her right fingers, noting the dark ink smudges soaked into her skin.

He turned back to the desk, his fingers absently tapping the wood top, and he noticed the ink in the inkwell was almost empty.

Interesting.

He checked in two of the drawers on the right side of the desk and found nothing. In the third drawer he opened, a stack of papers sat, the ink on them so full the sheets had warped with the wetness.

He pulled out the top several papers and lifted them closer to his face, studying the tight little script. Small and tiny, like Georgina had needed to write, but write a lot, so she had written as small as she could. Words flowed across the front, in between previously written lines, and up and down the edges on both sides of the paper until it was near to blacked out.

Slipped brandy into the punch at Lady Josten's ball.
Cut the ties holding Miss Thompson's dress in place after she cut Willow in front of Auntie's friends.
Let Willow walk into the alcove at Vauxhall Gardens alone, and Lord Fugal cornered her.

Had relations with Leroy.

Had relations with Leroy again. And again.

Cut Lord Lewson when he was nothing but nice to me.

Let Miss Sanders fight my battles.

Caused Miss Sanders death.

Stole shortbread from Cook's kitchen that she needed for the dinner party Auntie was hosting.

Lied to Willow about the babe.

Lied to Willow about relations with Leroy.

Knocked Janice's bonnet onto the ground and crushed it into the dirt with my heel after she laughed at Willow.

Attacked the clergyman.

Fake cried about attacking the clergyman to gain Auntie's forgiveness.

Let Silas help me after I lost the babe instead of insisting that he needed to leave me be.

Told mother's headstone I would trade baby Willow's life for hers, if only she would come back alive.

Insinuated to Silas there could possibly be a future, even encouraged it, when I knew full well there never would be.

Made fun of our Latin tutor's accent.

Didn't tell Auntie it was Willow and I that had made the mess of mud in the main fountain.

The statements went on and on. He picked up the next piece of paper. More of the same. And the third. Same. A stack deep into the drawer of page after page of the confessions.

Every perceived sin she'd ever committed in her life—
from birth onward—there, written and acknowledged.
Searching.

Georgina had spent these last two weeks searching for
answers. Answers on why she was here.

Why he had stolen her.

His heart twisted in his chest.

He had sent her into this madness, exactly as intended.

And it *was* madness.

Some of the sins so slight, they wouldn't even be called
sins. Especially the ones where she was simply defending her
sister.

He'd seen that in the time he'd followed her and
Willow at Toften Hall. How her ultimate goal in life had
been to make sure her sister was safe from harm, safe from
all the disparaging comments and looks.

She may not know how to knee a man in the ballocks,
but she did have that about her—a warrior's spirit when it
came to protecting her sister.

He dropped the papers back into the drawer and closed
it.

Turning around, he found Georgina awake and staring
at him.

The door was wide open, but she hadn't tried to sneak
out of the room while he was absorbed in reading what
she'd written.

He assumed she'd have reddened cheeks from what
they had done earlier, but there was no embarrassment on
her face. She owned her pleasure and that only made him
harder thinking about how she had twisted under his hands.

But it had been a mistake. A weakness on his part.

Josie. Remember Josie. Remember his *wife*.

Georgina pointed toward the food on the desk. "Still keeping Callum away from me?"

"He's sleeping, presumably. He was ready to tear you to pieces when he got back to the castle."

"I heard."

It was true—Callum had been yelling and he had been yelling right back—he'd even had to hold Callum back from coming up the stairs. Silas had seen him livid before, and a livid Callum was not safe to be around.

Georgina frowned. "You didn't let him come in here."

"No. I handed him a bottle of brandy and told him to go sulk elsewhere."

The frown on her face told him she didn't trust it—didn't trust him. And well she shouldn't. He'd made certain of that.

She nodded, more to herself, then to him, and her look dropped to the floor.

"Why did you let me kiss you?"

Her gaze jerked up to him. "Would you have stopped?"

"Yes. But you kissed me back, so I didn't stop. Why?"

Her shoulders lifted. "Because I'm stupid and I always seem to do what is obviously the wrong thing."

He exhaled a short guffaw. "I think we both know that's not the case."

Her mouth pulled into a frown and she looked down to the carpeting for a long moment. "I kissed you back because you were kissing me like you did at Toften Hall."

"How did I kiss you at Toften?"

"Like you wanted me, not my dowry." Her eyes lifted to him, her light blue irises soft, strangely warm with the memory bouncing about her head. "Like your body wanted mine so badly, you would have moved heaven and earth just to touch me for that one tiny moment in time. You kissed me like I was your next breath, the only thing that would keep you alive. That was how you kissed me at Toften. That was how you kissed me on that bed."

Bloody hell.

Now he wanted to throw her onto the bed again and finish what he started earlier.

Except he was in control at the moment. Not like he was when he was in here hours ago.

The softness in her eyes hardened into cold ice. "Don't fret. I will not make the mistake of letting it happen again."

Good. Exactly what he wanted to hear. For he was doing a shit job of keeping his hands off her.

But also…exactly what he didn't want to hear.

Not trusting what words his tongue would form, he inclined his head toward her and started to leave.

"You owe it to me."

Her words stopped his stride at the doorway and he turned around, his glare settling on her. "I owe you nothing."

She looked up at him, defiant, the tilt of her chin saying she wasn't about to back down. Not now. Not ever. No matter what he threw at her.

"No. You do. You owe me the reason. Do what you will with me for whatever my transgression was. But you owe me the reason you've locked me up here. I realize it is part of your sick game, to drive me mad with bewilderment. But I deserve to know what I've done to you to warrant what you have done to me."

"You killed her."

The words blurted out of his mouth even as he tried to keep them in.

She drew back in the chair, her face horrified. "What? Who? I've never, never even thought to—"

"You did." He cut her off. "I know all about it, so you can drop the act."

She scrambled to her feet, crossing the room to him. "What do you think you know? What do you think I did?"

"I know you told the coachman to kill her, he admitted exactly that to me."

Her cheeks crumpled up toward her eyes, her hand grabbing his arm. "What? I don't understand—what coachman? Told who what?"

"Leroy."

Her head snapped backward, her hand yanking away from him and she clasped onto her fingers like he had just singed her. "What? Leroy? No. Impossible. He's not a killer—why would you think he killed someone? He wouldn't hurt anyone."

His jawline pulled so tight, his jawbone was near to cracking. "Leroy admitted it to me—told me how her blood spilled onto the roadway when he killed her. How she struggled for breath."

Georgina stilled.

"Who did he kill?" Her voice had turned into a trace of a whisper, her face shifting to white.

"He killed Miss Sanders."

Her head shook, her feet shuffling backward, her hands up at him to ward off his words. "No—not Miss Sanders. Not Leroy." Her hand flew over her mouth. "Not Miss Sanders, not Leroy. No."

He advanced on her with every step she took away from him. "He did. He killed her on your orders. He shoved her in front of that carriage. In front of those horses."

"What?" Her body had started to shake, frantic, her eyes wild in confusion. "No, no. I never—"

"Don't lie about it now. I know. We know."

"No—" She turned from him and scrambled toward the bed, yanking out the chamber pot beneath it and retching into it. Retching again and again when she had very little in her stomach, only bile making it out.

His lip curled in disgust. He refused to feel sorry for her.

He waited until her retching stopped, her body drooping in exhaustion. "Your lover betrayed you. He told me everything."

Her head hung as she set the pot onto the floor, then sank onto the edge of the bed as she wiped the back of her trembling hand across her lips. "No—not Leroy. I cannot believe it. He couldn't have."

"Cannot believe that he betrayed you or that he killed her? He did both."

The tremble in her hand expanded until the whole of her, her limbs and torso were quivering. Her dazed look lifted to him. "Leroy—he killed Miss Sanders?"

He nodded.

"But I—I don't understand—I don't—she—she was my friend—she—why—" Georgina gasped a breath that turned into a sob as tears started to slip from her eyes.

Tears he wouldn't acknowledge, his heart a steel fortress against her.

Her breaths started heaving and she wrapped her arms around her belly, trying to stay upright even as her body started to sway. "No. Miss Sanders was my friend. He wouldn't have done that to her. He couldn't have."

"He did." His words were laced with venom. "He killed her because you asked him to. She was keeping you two apart."

Close to toppling over, she moved to the end of the bed, grabbing a hold of one of the bed posts, her only buoy in a tumultuous sea that wouldn't let her gain even a breath of air. "I—I never. We weren't together. I broke any connection to him a month before she died. We weren't together. I adored Miss Sanders."

"Don't lie about it now."

"You think…no…we…I was done with him." Her eyes squinted tightly closed as a desperate groan vibrated from her chest. "Done. After he questioned me—thought he wasn't the father—I was done with him. Done for good. I was going to have the child on my own."

"Play it all you want, Georgina, I know what you did."

Her hand slid down along the post and she slumped forward, her head bowed.

Silence.

Not acceptable.

He stepped toward her. "What? You have nothing to say now that the truth is out?"

She didn't move, didn't look up to him, didn't take a breath.

"Nothing?" The word slammed out into the room, demanding she look up at him. Face him for what she had wrought.

Excruciating moments slipped by, the air in the room thick with betrayal and tinged with a death that would not let either of them go.

"I don't." Her voice was beaten, so soft he could barely hear it. Her hand wrapped around the post dropped into her lap with a shiver. She didn't look up at him. "I don't have anything to say, because Leroy told you I did it, so to you, I will always be guilty. It doesn't matter what the truth of it was. He said it, so it was so. It became a truth even though it isn't. This world is for men and what they believe and I will never be able to prove my innocence because Leroy is dead."

Her shoulders lifted as she gasped a pitiful breath. "And you will never listen to me, believe me. So I am done. I give up. Keep me here in this room until I rot into dust and bones. I don't care. I cannot care anymore. I'm done. Everything is already lost, my babe, my sister, my future. Everything is gone, so I am done. There isn't anything left to fight for."

The sheer bleakness in her voice ripped a river of pity down the middle of him, but he ignored it.

He had to.

He walked out of room, locking the door behind him.

{ CHAPTER 21 }

"The key, Silas."

Silas looked up from the glass of brandy clutched in both of his hands in front of him. He'd been staring at the glass, his fifth one, for the last hour.

Callum stood in the doorway to his study, murder still on his face.

Silas's look dropped back down to the amber liquid. "Why the key? What do you think you're going to do to her?"

"Make her pay for escaping, for it's pretty obvious you didn't make her do so."

"She didn't know." He uttered the words out loud.

Said them for the world to hear, for the air to hold. Spoke them so they wouldn't be stuck in his head, repeating over and over since they had hours ago as he left his bedroom and locked the door.

Daphne pushed past Callum, moving into the study. "You're not going anywhere near her, Cal. You still need to calm down and you've been doing a shit job of it."

That was Daphne, the peacemaker only when she was forced into it. But she had a firm line when it came to honorable justice.

She moved to stand in front of Silas and crossed her arms. "And what in the hell did you just say?"

He let out a long sigh, then shifted his look to her. "She didn't know." Another heavy sigh lifted his chest. "Georgina didn't know what Leroy did."

"Just because she didn't know what he did, doesn't mean she didn't ask him to do it."

With his forehead angled down, his look pierced her. "She didn't ask him to do it."

"No." Daphne shook her head. "She did—you said so. That's the whole damn reason you brought us here."

"I was fucking wrong."

Daphne's lip curled. "No. I'm not accepting that. She's a liar and she's playing upon your sympathies."

"No."

"And he's drinking," Callum grumbled.

Daphne looked to Callum and then pinned her gaze on Silas. "Exactly. She's a liar."

Silas set his glass onto the round inlaid marquetry maple side table next to him and rubbed his hand over his eyes, then pinched the bridge of his nose. "You didn't see her. You didn't hear her. She didn't know about Leroy. Didn't even know what he did. Didn't know what he planned to do."

Daphne scoffed a laugh. "And you're thinking with your cock instead of your heart. When you should be thinking about Josie."

Silas jolted up onto his feet, towering over Daphne as he took a step toward her. "Don't you dare say I'm not thinking about Josie. I haven't thought about a damn thing other than finding her killer since she died."

"Well, you found her. She's upstairs sitting in your room. In your bed. And you're telling me you're not thinking with your cock?"

A growl escaped him and he took another step toward Daphne, meeting her head-on. "I said Georgina didn't have anything to do with her murder, and I meant it. I know it."

"Do you?"

"Yes."

"How?" Daphne asked, not backing down.

"Because she knows exactly what I think she did and she's given up. Given up on everything."

Daphne's eyebrows lifted. "That sounds exactly like someone that *is* guilty."

"No. She's tired. Exhausted. Beaten down into this. Guilty liars don't give up. They cling to their lies until the very end. They need to, it's how they rationalize their actions."

"Or are you just rationalizing now?"

His hands curled into fists. "I know it in my gut, Daphne. I was wrong. Leroy—that coachman—he was lying when he said Georgina had anything to do with Josie's death. He was trying to clear his guilt before he met his maker."

She hissed out an aggravated groan. "I'm not staying for this. You yanked us up here for justice for Josie and now you're telling us you were wrong? For if you were wrong…" Her head shook and her hands flew up at her sides. "I'm leaving. Do what you want with the girl, but just know that no matter what side the truth lies on, you sure as hell haven't honored Josie's memory."

She stomped toward the door, looking at Callum. "You coming or staying?"

Callum looked at Silas for a long moment, his jaw ticking. "I'm coming."

He turned and followed Daphne out the door.

His teeth clenched, Silas stared at the empty door for long minutes.

Daphne was right. If he was right about Georgina's involvement, it was a mistake to let her off the hook.

Except he was wrong. Wrong and he knew it.

He'd listened to some soulless killer because he'd been out for blood, more blood than Leroy's alone, for that man's blood hadn't sated his thirst for vengeance.

Now he was facing the grievous error he'd made.

One he could never make right.

{ CHAPTER 22 }

Georgina woke up early, before the sun had even thought to spread its first rays.

The darkness still thick around her, she noticed immediately the air in the room was different.

Her fingers fumbled in the dark for the candle next to the bed as she shifted her feet to the floor. She grabbed the candlestick and shuffled her way across the room to the fireplace, where coals were still glowing from the fire she'd made last night, trying to ease away the chill that had set deep into her bones after Silas had left the room.

The chill of utter defeat. She would die here.

It all made sense now, and that was the only outcome.

Silas thought she'd killed Miss Sanders. Miss Sanders was a guardian. Silas, Callum, Daphne—all of them had to be guardians. It only made sense. They were guardians out for vengeance, out for her blood.

She couldn't even blame them, for there was no limit to what she would do if someone killed Willow. She would learn how to use a damn dagger, and she would kill that person without a second thought of hell and brimstone.

Though she, on the other hand, would make damn sure she was sending the right person to hell.

An integrity Silas and his fellow guardians were sorely lacking.

She dipped the wick into the coals and gently blew on it until the wick lit. Holding the candlestick up, she stood and turned around.

The door to the room was open.

Open.

That was why the air was different. Not the stuffy, heavy air that had suffocated her for more than a fortnight.

Not quite believing it, especially after what Silas had told her yesterday, she crept cautiously toward the door, holding the candlestick in front of her.

Her skin prickled as she waited for a sword blade to come swinging at her neck or an arrow to whizz straight into her chest.

At the threshold to the sitting room, she paused.

No one.

No one sitting. No one sleeping. The room was empty.

A trap?

Or liberation?

She took one tiny step into the room and wasn't decapitated or shot. So she took another step and then another.

The door to the sitting room was also open.

A clear message.

Leave while she could.

She popped her head into the dark hallway, looking both directions as far as the light allowed. Again, no one.

She moved out into the hallway, then thought to look down. She couldn't rightly escape in Silas's wrecked clothes and no shoes.

To the right and across the hallway, she found several open doorways. The first room was empty of everything, even furniture, but the second room was elegant, clearly feminine.

She stepped in and went to the delicate armoire on the far wall. A number of dresses were hanging inside and she grabbed the closest one to her. She went over to the bed, quickly stripping off Silas's clothes and dragging on the dress. It fit reasonably well, the skirt was a touch long, but she could take care to not trip on the hem.

The dress in place, Georgina twisted her arms behind her to secure the buttons up her spine as she went back to the armoire and searched in the bottom. Boots. Perfect.

In short order, she had the roomy boots on and had found a shawl, wrapped it around her, and was moving down through the castle. Her heart madcap in her chest, she took the same route she had run down when she had escaped past Callum, and was outside within minutes.

Into the woods in the opposite direction she took last time, she didn't slow her speedy gait until she stumbled onto a roadway just as the first rays of the sun started to glow over the countryside.

The promise of a new dawn expanded the spark that she had been afraid to stoke in her chest when she'd seen the open doorway. A spark of hope.

East.

London.

She set her feet in that direction and started walking.

{ CHAPTER 23 }

Shit.

She was wearing Josie's dress.

Josie's favorite dark purple dress, so very durable and with hidden pockets all about.

Though, what should he have expected?

Georgina had been wearing his clothes last night. It wasn't like she could venture out into the world like that, or in that thin shift he'd brought her back to the castle in.

At least she was far off the road, walking along just within the line of trees that followed the cut of the roadway. Smarter than her last escape attempt.

Small favor that the road had been empty since he'd taken off from the castle to look for her—he'd guessed to the east and he'd been right.

He drew closer and Georgina looked over her shoulder at the sound of his horse's hooves on the roadway. For a moment, she paused, looking ready to bolt into the woods, but then she clearly recognized him.

She turned around and kept walking. Her feet drifting through the low hanging fog that hadn't yet dissipated with the day.

Silas nicked his horse into a trot to catch up to her.

Once he was in line with her, he slowed his horse to the speed of her gait. "You rose before daybreak."

She didn't afford him a glance. "I did."

"You never do that."

Her feet stomping harder into the ground as she walked, she looked to him, haughty scorn lacing her eyes. "You know so much about me?"

"You've been under my watch at Yarstone for weeks. Daphne and Cal reported everything, so I know quite a bit about you."

"You know nothing of me." Her stare set forward and her pace quickened as she dodged inward around a large oak tree.

Silas swung his leg over his horse and dismounted, grabbing the reins and walking in pace with her. "I know you don't rise before daybreak."

"I did today."

"Where are you walking to, Georgina?"

"London."

He kicked a rock out of his path. "London?"

"Yes."

He took several steps in silence. "Or you could come back to the castle with me."

"No." She looked at him, her words biting out. "Just force me if you're going to force me to come back. Just get on with it."

"I'm not going to force you to do anything."

"No?" She scoffed a chuckle that echoed through the trees. "That is laughable."

"I'm not. I'm not here to force you. Not here to make you do anything." Pulling his horse along with him, he veered down the side of the roadway, closer to the path along the woods she was walking. "So, you think you are going to walk to London?"

"Yes." Her stare set forward again. "Home. I'm going home. No matter what it costs me, I'm going home."

"You cannot make it back to London on foot."

"I can."

He held back a sigh bubbling in his chest. He deserved all of this. All of this and worse. So while he wanted to grab her and throw her onto the horse, he kept his steps light, nonthreatening beside her. "But what will you eat? Where will you sleep?"

Her shoulders lifted in a shrug. "I have my body. Apparently, that is my only worth, so I will use it to make my way."

His gut dropped out from his center, the mere thought of another man touching her sending a rock through his belly.

Anger he couldn't control riled his voice. "Don't you dare think to set yourself in a position where you will sell your body."

"Why do you even care?" Her words spat out into the early morning air. "If you aren't going to drag me back into that room, then just let me go. Let me go and never think on me again."

Hell. That would be so easy. So damn easy to let her go. It would also be the coward's way out. And he wasn't a coward.

He made the mistake and now he had to face it.

Not to mention the fact that he would never be able to not think on her. No matter what happened here, in this moment, she would haunt his mind until his last breath.

He cleared his throat. "Except that I do care, Georgina. I care quite a bit."

The toe of her left foot tripped on something under the fog and she stumbled a step, then glanced at him.

"Come back to the castle."

"No."

His patience stretched to the point of snapping, especially when he knew how this was going to end for her if she kept on this course of action. She would find herself, somewhere along the route, in the exact same position he found her in at the brothel. The mere thought of it turning the world around him red, making him want to destroy everything and everyone from here to London just to keep her safe.

He did exactly what he'd told himself he wasn't about to do. He dropped the reins of his horse and darted inward to grab Georgina's arm.

Her feet yanked to a stop and she instantly tried to twist her arm out of his grip.

"Stop—just stop, Georgina." He didn't let her escape his hold, his face closing in on hers. "I don't want you attacked. I don't want you raped. I don't want another man's grimy hands to touch you, and that's exactly what will happen if you are foolishly determined to continue on. Come back to Yarstone with me."

Her eyes went to pinpricks on him. "Come back so you can lock me up again?"

"Come back so I can deliver you properly to London."

"What?" Her head shook, her eyes searching his face. "What are you telling me? You cannot—"

"I believe you. I'm telling you I believe you. You didn't ask Leroy to murder Miss Sanders. I believe you and I will deliver you back to London. I swear it."

Her jaw slipped open and in silence, her stare ate into him for a long breath. "And I should trust you why?"

He eased his hold on her arm, but didn't back off from where his face was only inches away from hers. "You shouldn't. Honestly, you should have never trusted me, but you did. And I took full advantage of that. All to your detriment. I did that and I'm sorry. More sorry than you will ever know. I made a grievous error when I was in a rage and my mind was consumed with vengeance and you were the extraneous damage I didn't realize I was creating."

He stopped, shaking his head, the weight of her stare near to taking his breath away. "All of that is unforgivable, I know that. But in this…this moment, this place that we find ourselves. In this, please, just let me make this right— as right as I can."

Her eyes closed, a flicker of uncertainty running across her face as she exhaled. Her eyes opened and she looked past him toward his horse at the side of the road, munching on grass. "And if I do come back with you?"

"You won't regret it, I promise."

"You realize I trust you as far as I can throw you?" Her look ran up and down him. "And I can't even pick you up?"

"I'm not asking for your trust. I'm just asking for your time. We go back to the castle, I'll arrange a proper carriage

and a driver and I will take you to London. It is only time, not trust, that I ask of you."

She met his gaze, uncertainty palpitating in her blue irises.

She didn't want to do it. That was obvious.

So he willed her, willed her with everything he had to just accept it. To accept his help.

She nodded.

A victory.

A small one.

But a victory nonetheless.

{ CHAPTER 24 }

The cook set a plate full of sizzling bacon next to eggs, rolls, and preserves on the table in front of Georgina.

The smell invading her nostrils and setting her mouth to water, Georgina picked up her fork, ready to dive in without restraint. This was the first hot meal she'd had in weeks.

The first bite hit her mouth and Georgina moaned, swallowed and looked up to the cook.

"This is delicious, thank you so much for making it so late in the morning. Silas was rude when he set you onto the task and rushed off, as he did not introduce you."

"Mrs. Lindern, ma'am." She gave Georgina a nod. "His lordship is not accustomed to introducing me to anyone."

"Yet I assume you know Callum and Daphne?"

"Them, I know."

"Are they still here?"

"No."

Georgina nodded to herself. "Beyond that? Do you know anything of what happens here at Yarstone?"

Mrs. Lindern's lips pulled to the side, wrinkling her face as she shook her head. "I don't ask and I don't talk of this place. It's the condition of my employment."

Georgina nodded as she took another bite of the perfectly seasoned eggs. "I imagine. Do you have to do that often, not ask any questions?"

She exhaled a laugh. "I am not at liberty to say, ma'am. Though I will say, I haven't served a soul here at this table, well, ever."

"No one eats in here?"

"No. I usually leave the food in the kitchen and it is grabbed when needed. If I am making a hot meal, his lordship likes to eat in his study at his side table." She paused, looking around the cold cavernous room. "Not one for formality, his lordship, though I would say it would be lonely eating in here."

Georgina glanced up at the high stone walls surrounding her. The room was meant for twenty, thirty, fifty people eating in it. Not one. She was at the end of the castle's main hall, next to the enormous rounded fireplace with a comically small fire sitting in the middle of it. Grey everywhere she looked. A hall like this was usually covered with tapestries and banners to lend the feeling of warmth, but this space was just cold.

It did have one outstanding feature, though, the majestic arched wooden beams that spanned across the wooden ceiling. Gargoyles were carved into the ends of the large blocks of wood dotted along the beams. Ever watching. Ever judging. Ever laughing at the folly of humans.

It would be lonely in here. She hadn't seen Silas's study, but it had to have more warmth than this space. Odd that he had left her in here. Or maybe it was because this was the closest room to the kitchens for Mrs. Lindern.

"Would ye like anything else, ma'am?"

Georgina took a sip of the tea the cook had brought in and shook her head. "No, all of this is wonderful, thank you."

Mrs. Lindern nodded, then disappeared through the doorway on the sidewall next to the fireplace.

Georgina continued to eat, the tinging of her fork on the plate echoing up into the rafters. Lonely, indeed.

Though it didn't take much effort to ignore the feeling. Not when her belly actually wanted to have food in it.

Whether or not Silas had been honest in wanting to take her back to London—and she had serious doubts about what was to happen next—this meal, in this moment, was a pleasure she wasn't going to deny herself.

She'd long since finished her food and was staring at the ceiling, separating the above gargoyles into playful, scheming, happy, thoughtful or just plain evil categories, when Silas walked in though the main doors at the far end of the hall.

"You ate?" he asked, his boots clunking along the wide stones set in the floor.

She lifted her empty plate toward him. "Mrs. Lindern is an excellent cook."

A smile quirked the edges of his lips. "That she is."

He stopped along the grotesquely long table that probably hadn't moved from this spot since the Middle Ages and held out his hand to her. "Come with me."

Without making motion to grab it, she looked at his hand, then to his face. "Where to?"

"Only upstairs to one of the chambers. The coach is set to be here in an hour and I want us to be ready."

She wanted to hate him—she *did* hate him.

But anytime he was in front of her, the hate refused to manifest like she knew it should. She should be screaming at him. Slapping him. Hitting him.

But she didn't have it in her. She didn't possess hate like that. And she couldn't manifest it out of thin air like she knew she should.

Even if Silas deserved every bit of hate she had in her. She couldn't hate him. Not truly. Not when her body betrayed her at every turn, wanting his in some guttural, ancient way she didn't understand and couldn't control.

Another failing to add to the list.

So she lifted her arm and cautiously set her hand in his. His fingers softly wrapped around her hand, enveloping it. A shock of a touch to her system and she almost yanked her hand away. She'd been hating this man for weeks now, and to have that gentle of a touch from him perplexed her.

He gave her a tentative smile, almost like he couldn't believe she'd actually taken his hand.

She went to her feet and he led her through the castle, not letting her hand go. It wasn't until they were at the threshold of the room that she had gone into that morning to find clothes that he dropped her hand.

He motioned her inward. "You'll need proper clothing for the journey."

She looked down, running her hand along the front of the simple dark violet dress she'd found and put on before she'd left. It was simple but functional, not that she took time to go through the wardrobe earlier—she had just wanted to get out of the castle in one piece. "What I'm wearing is not appropriate?"

"You need to arrive like you left. In finery that befits you. It will present better."

She inhaled a breath, not wanting to let her mind go there—what it would be like to return to her aunt and uncle at this point after being gone for so long. The disappointment on their faces. They loved her, yes, but both of them had wanted so much for her and Willow to find fine matches and give them grandnieces and nephews— heirs to the family legacy.

That dream was dead.

At least her part to play in it. She was damaged goods and everyone knew it. There would have been no way to cover up her disappearance for this long.

She glanced up at Silas.

He looked...hopeful. How odd.

To ruin her and then think he could return her in a pretty dress with no damage done.

She stepped away from him and into the room, walking toward the armoire she had found the violet dress in.

"No, that holds the serviceable dresses. Come in here and look." He moved across the room to a skinny door on the side of the room and opened it. From her angle, she could see dress after dress in the smaller adjoining chamber.

She glanced at him as she stepped past him. "Whose room is this?"

He stilled, his eyes going downward for a short second and then he met her gaze. "It was Miss Sanders's room."

Georgina gasped, her feet stopping in the doorway, her arm pressed against his. Her neck twisted as she stared up at him, her voice a whisper. "Miss Sanders?"

He gave one nod.

"But she was a guardian…" She looked into the dressing chamber and then back to him, her brow furrowed. "She was a guardian, why would she have a suite here?"

"She was also my wife."

A battering ram to her belly, Georgina staggered a step away from him, her spine cracking into the frame of the doorway. "Your…your wife?"

He nodded. "My wife."

The world went blurry in front of her and she stood, stunned, for how long she wasn't sure, as all feeling left her limbs, her head bobbing like she was floating, untethered to anything around her.

She heaved a breath. Then another. "Miss Sanders was your wife?"

"She was." His voice caught on the words.

Damn, he was too close to her. Suffocating. Too damn close.

Her hand went up, landing on his chest and she had to push against him to make her feet move. She shuffled back into the main room toward the bed, landing on her backside before she lost the last bit of feeling in her legs and crumpled to the floor.

Her stare stayed on the floor, the world still a blur around her. "What…" She had to stop, swallowing down the hard lump wedged in her throat. "What was her name?

She would never tell us. Said she couldn't. It was a rule. Was she even Miss Sanders?"

It took him a long moment to answer her. "No. Miss Sanders was her childhood governess."

She looked up to him as he moved out into the main room, stopping in front of her to look down on her. "Her name was Josie."

His voice caught on her name and he coughed, clearing his throat. Abruptly, he took a step back, then turned and went to the door leading out to the hallway. "Pick out one of the finer dresses in the wardrobe and put it on, then we can be on our way. I'll leave you to it."

He stepped out into the corridor, pulling the door closed behind him, but leaving it slightly ajar.

A clear message.

She wasn't locked in.

As soon as he was out of sight, she crumpled forward, her face landing in her hands.

Miss Sanders—Josie—was his wife. His *wife*.

And he had thought she had killed her.

Killed his wife.

Damn Leroy.

Damn him to hell for that's surely where he was burning right now.

Damn herself for ever looking at that bastard with stupid, naïve, blushing eyes.

So many mistakes. So many idiotic mistakes she'd made.

She sat, overwhelmed for what seemed like ages until she realized Silas would return soon.

Her legs two heavy stumps, she wobbled into the adjoining dressing chamber and forced herself to look at the dresses.

All clothes that looked like they would fit Miss Sanders—Josie.

Josie.

She'd had a name—a beautiful name the entire time Georgina had known her—and Georgina never knew it.

Her fingers lifted, touching the muslin, the silk, fingering the purple trim on the day dresses. Josie had liked that color. All the dresses her uncle paid for when he thought Josie was a dear old friend of his nieces were purple. A sad, melancholy purple. But it was her favorite.

She stopped in the corner of the wardrobe in front of a violet concoction. A day dress, perfect for visiting or the market, but fine enough to let the world know the owner wouldn't stoop to actually carry anything that was bought. A delicate layer of light purple trim hugged the bodice and sleeves of the dress.

Josie's favorite dress.

Georgina's fingers moved without thought and she stripped off the simple walking dress she wore and let it fall to the floor, then carefully set her fingers along the silk edges of the other dress, fluffing it out so the skirt went wide.

She put on a shift and then slipped the dress onto her body, letting it settle.

Too much.

All of it, too much.

Tears started to fall. Fall for her friend. Fall for Silas losing his wife. Fall for her sister. Fall for herself.

All of it, so bitterly unfair.

Her legs buckled and she slid down, a puddle on the floor in Josie's favorite dress. Favorite because it was the one she always wore when she could. The one with three special pockets to hold daggers ready to pull.

Georgina had more than once seen Josie pull those blades on gentlemen that weren't exactly gentlemen—most of them trying to corner her or Willow in some alcove.

Always protecting her.

While she had been too blind to see that Josie was the one that needed to be protected. Josie was the one with a target on her back.

Footsteps echoed into the main room and for the life of her, Georgina couldn't stop the tears before Silas stepped into the dressing chamber.

His black boots stopped in front of her and his voice came quiet, hesitant. "Georgina?"

She couldn't look up at him, her voice hiccupping. "I don't know what in the hell I'm supposed to do."

He dropped down, sitting on his heels. "Why the tears?" He reached out, his thumb wiping along her cheek, clearing the wetness with the softest touch.

"All of this I deserve." She looked up to him, his face blurry through her tears. "I was the one that had the affair with Leroy. I set it all in motion. I stupidly put myself and Willow in danger with Lord Fugal and his cousins. Me. I did that. And Josie is dead because of me—and you—you lost your wife. It doesn't even matter if I never told him to do it. Leroy did it because of me. Because I let him into our lives."

His hand pulled away from her face.

Her head shook, her gaze dropping away from him in shame as she took a wavering breath. "And now I am ruined—there is no coming back from disappearing for weeks. I have no future. I have ruined everything and everyone around me. And I don't know what to do."

"Marry me."

Her look whipped upward, the tears draining away in disbelief. How could he possibly think that was what she wanted to hear? She stared at him, her eyes narrowing, a scoff in her throat. "I'm not your problem."

"No, you're my choice." Both of his hands reached out, sliding along the opposite sides of her jaw as his thumbs swiped away the remnants of her tears. "Marry me."

"No."

"I ruin you, I marry you. It is only fair." His hazel eyes, tinged with purple from the reflections of the dresses around him, bored into her. "Let us make right one thing in this madness. It is the only thing we can do now."

Her heart constricting in her chest, she nodded, knowing it wasn't right, knowing he didn't really want her.

But she nodded.

It was her only option.

{ Chapter 25 }

"Oh."

Silas paused on the lane outside the coaching inn in Northampton, looking down to her next to him. "What is it?"

"Nothing. I forgot my satchel in the carriage." Georgina half-turned to search down the street, but the carriage they'd travelled here in had already turned down the cross lane toward the stables for the night. She waved her hand in the air thick with drizzle. "But it is of no bother. This is our first stop so I can make do without it, the most important thing was the hairbrush, but my fingers will do in a pinch. They have for a while now."

Silas winced.

She hadn't meant the end of her comment as a barb, but it still stung him and she knew it. Though she wasn't sure if that pleased her or not. She'd gone through the day, her nerves and mind tattered with all that had happened and she still didn't know how she felt about anything.

Silas glanced around, his eyes wary for a moment, but then he appeared to relax. It was a busy enough street with plenty of people quickly walking to and from the shops that lined the road. Little danger lurking about.

She'd noticed that about him during the day, how he always had an eye out to their surroundings, like she needed protecting at every corner, when she didn't. Away from

London and the overzealous suitors of the *ton*, there was no threat to her person.

He took her elbow and guided her to the front of the coaching inn and under an awning that offered a dry spot from the drizzle quickly turning into rain. "Wait here. I'll go retrieve it."

Her fingers curled around his arm. "Truly, it is not a bother. We still have at least three more nights until Scotland. I can make myself presentable before then."

He chuckled, his head tilting to the side as his eyes raked her over. "You're more than presentable now. And I honestly cannot imagine you getting any less so."

The heat in his eyes set the blood in her veins to pound harder, and her breath caught in her throat.

"But I will still go and fetch your bag."

She released her hold on his arm and nodded.

Better that she had a moment to herself. The entire carriage ride that day had her on edge. Silas had been nothing but charming—exactly as he had been at Toften Hall—and it had set a nervous flutter into her belly, for she'd been deceived by him once before. What if all of this was a ruse? Just a way to get her farther and farther from her home?

She'd been fooled by him before. Fooled by his fun banter and witty observations and his questions about what she thought and his hazel eyes that today were tinged with a vibrant blue.

The flutter in her belly was a warning. A warning she needed to heed, instead of falling into the same trap again and again with the man.

Waiting in front of the coaching inn, she looked around, observing this area of the town. It was bustling, even in the drizzling rain. A number of wagons moved through town, as well as a few carriages and phaetons. Lots of people walking with packages. It must be market day, though she hadn't seen a market square on the way into the town.

She looked down, nudging the mud by the toe of her boot—correction—by the toe of Josie's boot she had borrowed.

Josie.

Her heart went heavy in her chest.

Silas's wife. His *wife*.

His dead wife.

For all she knew she should hate Silas for what he'd done to her—kidnapping, deciding she was guilty without bothering to learn the truth of the matter—she was having a hard time stoking the anger in her heart.

He had thought she had killed his wife.

Thought it because of a lie by Leroy—and to what end on his part? Did Leroy think he would escape persecution if he could pin Josie's death on her? And now she couldn't even confront the bastard about it.

Her eyes closed, her head shaking to herself. How could she ever have trusted Leroy? How could she ever have let him touch her in the first place?

So *many* damn mistakes.

The thought repeated in her head and a festering trickle of foreboding slithered into her mind just as a man stopped in front of her. A big man. His clothes were rough, with an

ill-fitting brown coat stretched tight at the seams over his shoulders. He had a flat face, like he'd been smashed in the face with a board again and again as a child.

She looked upward, a hesitant smile on her face. "Can I do something for you, sir? Should I not be standing here?" She motioned over her shoulder. "I could go inside and wait if I am in the way."

"Ye waiting for the man ye got out of the coach with?"

Her brow furrowed and she looked to her right where Silas had disappeared after the coach. This man had seen them alight the carriage? "Yes. I am just waiting for my companion and we—"

A second man, practically a twin to the first one in size and girth except with three missing front teeth, stepped in front of her gaze and the two of them angled together, boxing her in against the wall next to the door. "Ye could come with us, that's what ye could do for us."

A shiver ran down her spine as her head snapped back. "No, I don't think I will. I think I will stay right here until my companion returns." Her hands went flat onto the outer stone wall of the inn and she shuffled to her left, trying to work her way toward the door.

The first man wedged a foot into her path, blocking her with his leg. "Yer companion ain't what he says he is. Ye need to come with us for yer own safety."

She looked to her right, then to her left. Only the masses of the two men in front of her. Closing in and suffocating.

Tucking her head, she turned fully to her left and tried to barrel past the man.

His arm went up and she rammed into it, the force of her body jerking to a stop and knocking the breath out of her.

She gasped, trying to scream. Only a squeak came out. No air in her lungs. She swallowed, trying to get her breath as she pushed at the man's arm locking her in place.

The air shifted behind her and she heard a sickening *thunk.*

Flesh—bone—hitting stone.

She twisted just in time to see the second thug slumping against the building, Silas's fist gripping the back of his skull. Silas released him and he slid down the building, dropping to the ground, blood covering his forehead.

The first flat-faced brute grabbed her arm, yanking her in front of him, but Silas was quicker, a fist flying right past her head and into the man's jaw. Another crack that made her stomach roll.

The man stumbled backward, but the blow wasn't enough for him to drop his death grip on her shoulder, and he dragged her backward with him.

She twisted, trying to wedge out of his hold, but his nails dug harder into her shoulder.

Silas rounded him in the next instant and snaked his arm around the man's neck, choking him.

That did it. It took several long seconds, but the brute released her, his fingers gradually losing grip. Silas grunted as the man struggled against him, but his lock on the man's neck was brutal, not allowing him any air.

The man's arms slowed in their frantic swings backward to reach Silas, and his eyes closed, his body going limp.

When the full weight of him dropped with gravity, Silas released his hold around the man's neck.

The brute at his feet, Silas looked to her, a pulsating rage rolling off of him in waves. "Did they hurt you?"

She shook her head, not able to trust that she could coherently string any words together. A quick glance around and she was taken aback that no one walking the streets had taken any note of what had just happened. Or maybe Silas had just gone about it so quietly, that no one thought to look.

Silent violence.

She swallowed hard.

He grabbed her hand, then thought the better of it and reached out, plucking her off the ground and swinging her over the brute slumped on the ground between them. He set her down next to him, but kept an arm wrapped around her waist as he steered her toward the door.

The dangerous air palpitating around him enveloped her, pricking all her senses and not allowing her to gain a proper breath. Primal. He was utterly primal at the moment, ready to set anyone trying to touch her on fire.

And she didn't hate it.

He paused at the doorway and looked down at her, his stare steely. "One room tonight, then?"

Her eyes wide, her mouth dry, she nodded.

{ CHAPTER 26 }

"Your hands are still shaking."

"I am fine." Georgina dropped them into her lap, hiding them under the table. Deuced hard to eat that way, but she had to get control of herself. Silas already thought her weak—unable to defend herself. He'd said as much after getting her out of the whorehouse.

She wasn't about to add uncontrollable quivers onto that list.

"You don't have to hide from me, Georgina." He picked up his wine glass from the table in their room at the coaching inn and took a sip.

"You want to see my hands shaking?" She glanced down into her lap, then looked up at him. "I don't want to see my hands shaking."

"I don't want to see it either, but if it is reality, then I want to know. I want to know what is going on in your mind. In your body."

Her shoulders lifted. "I have never understood the cruelty that existed outside of Grovewick Abbey. Yes, I knew people who were cruel to Willow—but those barbs were always words and disgusted looks. We could guard against those. None of it was a physical threat. London was so different. I didn't understand that as a woman I was a possession—just a piece of meat to be manhandled. That men would use and abuse me as they saw fit and not think

twice on it. That my actual life could be in danger." She drew in a warbled breath, her look settling on him. "How do you do it? How do you crush two huge brutes into the ground as you did and not feel a flicker of fear?"

"They were touching you." He leaned over the table, setting his glass down as his look sank into her. "No one touches you. And if they are…well, fear is not a course I would take."

The harsh possessiveness in his tone cut her to the marrow and she had to force her eyes to continue to meet his rather than cower away. His hazel eyes had clouded to a menacing grey ever since he had found her corned by those two men, and they'd been that way the entire time it took to get to the room and for food to be brought up.

She'd seen the cruelty he was capable of first hand when it had been directed at her. But to see this—to see his fury on behalf of her—was unsettling.

She managed to hold his gaze. "Except that was more than lack of fear. You knew how to take care of those men so efficiently, I hardly had time to blink and they were down."

His head angled to the side. "You need to learn to protect yourself. We will start on that."

She gave him a slight nod, pausing as she edged her tongue toward the question that had haunted her since she'd first asked it. "Are you truly one of the Guardians of the Bones?"

He leaned back in his chair, his fingers toying with the unused fork by his plate. "Do you need to know?"

"I do. I'm about to marry you. I would like to know what, exactly, I am getting into."

He sighed as he flipped the fork over a few more times, then sat up straight, setting his elbows on the table and leaning forward. He'd stripped off his coat and waistcoat when they'd entered the room and now just wore his lawn shirt, rolled up at the sleeves. The cords of muscles along his forearms twitched with every slight movement. "Yes. I am a Guardian."

Her jaw dropped with an intake of breath. She had assumed it, but to hear it from his own lips startled her. "You and Miss Sanders—Josie—were both Guardians of the Bones? And you are also the Marquess of Atwell?"

"Correct."

"But…how does that work—you were married but kept it a secret? To be a guardian is to live a covert life, as I understand it."

"People who needed to know, did. But yes, to society, I am a bachelor. Quite a catch I am, I am told."

She laughed. "But Josie—I don't understand, why did she still work for the Guardians if you were married, and for that matter, why do you work for the Guardians?"

His lips pursed for a moment as darkness flashed across his eyes. "It's how we survived for a long time. Josie did the work because it was what she loved. What her purpose in life was. I worked for the Guardians—still do—because I would have followed Josie into anything. The Guardians are the ones that arranged the title for me to take on, as it pays for us to have people in all levels of society. I was the lucky one that fit the bill."

Her brows lifted. "Because you are handsome and charming and can lie to everyone you meet?"

"Exactly." He grinned, so very different than how his face had been twisted in hate when he stole her away from Toften Hall. It was jarring how easily he had reverted to the man she had known at Toften Hall, except it had started to make sense now that she knew everything he was, was a lie.

Yet still, the grin on his face, easy and relaxed, sent a flutter into her chest. A flutter she tried to ignore. "So you were not born into the title?"

"Far from it. I was a stableboy for the first thirteen years of my life."

"No." She shook her head, her eyes narrowing as she tried to read his face. "Are you lying now?"

The grin slipped from his lips. "No."

"I am to believe that?"

"I realize that it will be a long time before you believe anything I have to say. I realize and understand it." His head fell back and he looked at the ceiling for a long moment, then his gaze dropped back to her. "I didn't meet you at Toften Hall."

"What? Yes, we did. You, I would have remembered meeting anywhere and we met at Toften."

"Well, yes, that's when *we* did meet. But I had been shadowing you for months before that. Ever since Josie died. I came into this in order to find out who killed her, but I was also determined to finish Josie's job with you and your sister. She would have wanted me to. And I did a shit job at it because my mind was not in its right state. I'm

sorry that I didn't see what a threat Lord Fugal was to you
and Willow."

Her body froze, her hands tightening into fists in her
lap. "You—you have been following us for months?"

"Yes."

"For months?" She stared at him. Only honesty in his
eyes. Or so she thought. "Months you were following us
about?"

He nodded. "It was easier to pinpoint the men that
were about to make untoward advances upon you that way.
I was at the parties and the balls—on the fringes so I wasn't
noticed—and every time a connection wanted to introduce
us, I made up an excuse to leave."

She exhaled a breath. "For months?"

"Yes." The right side of his lips twitched into the
slightest smile.

What was entertaining to him was disconcerting to
her. He'd been shadowing her for months and she hadn't the
slightest clue.

She blinked hard, attempting to push that thought—
her utter lack of awareness—to the back of her mind. "Why
did you finally arrange an introduction to me?"

"I couldn't stay away any longer."

"Stay away from what?"

"You."

Her breath hiccupped in her chest. This was too much.
Far too much.

Remember. He'd kidnapped her. Ruined her. Had
apparently been stalking her for months.

And she was on her way to marry the bastard.

She looked down to her plate and moved to pick up her fork, shaking hand or not. She started shoveling food into her mouth, one bite after another, all in effort to not look at him. To not acknowledge what he'd just said.

He let her eat in silence, taking a few bites of the roast and the beets, sipping his wine, but mostly just waiting for her to finish eating.

Her plate only half empty, she couldn't shove another bite in for how small her stomach had shriveled during the last few weeks at Yarstone.

She took a sip of wine, finally gaining the fortitude to look at him again. His eyes met hers immediately, as she knew they would. He'd been staring at her the entire time she'd been eating and trying to avoid him. "I don't know what to say to you. All of this is just…a lot to take in."

He stood up from the table and went to the fireplace, using the fire poker to stoke the fire that been reduced to low flames.

Satisfied, he set the poker by the fire and turned around to her, but didn't move toward his seat. "Tell me, at Toften Hall, before I took you away to Yarstone, did you think about it?"

She set her wine glass down and looked at him. "Think about what?"

"Us. Did you consider me, at all?"

"Consider you?" She scoffed a laugh, fidgeting and looking over her shoulder at the sole bed in the room. Best not to think on that at the moment.

Her fingers lifted, running along the edge of her hairline as her gaze shifted back to him. "I wasn't in the position to consider you. You know the exact position I was in. I was looking to protect my babe, nothing more."

"To that end, you didn't consider finding yourself in a compromising position with me to force a union?"

She sighed, shaking her head. "No one deserves to be made a cuckhold. I could never do that, live a life of lies like that."

He stared at her for a long moment, judging her words, then nodded. "So you never imagined for a moment that you weren't with child and thought about us? We were a match. That much was obvious in the time we spent together. And you never considered it, not even after you lost the babe?"

"What do you want me to say, Silas?" Heat started to creep up along her neck. "That I looked at you and my heart beat faster? That I always sought you out to talk to at Toften Hall because you are funny and kind? That I knew before I even met you properly, that you were the exact type of man I wanted as my husband?"

His mouth quirked to the side. "How did you know I was that exact type of man before you even met me?"

She scooted her chair away from the table and turned it toward him, leaning on the left arm rest. "Easy. You danced with Willow first thing at Toften Hall. Then you were told about her peculiarity by the Brighton twins. And then you still talked with Willow, still danced with her again. Men don't do that once they know—at least not the men we've met during the season. Your actions alone told me everything I needed to know about you. Lies or not, you

were an easy man to like. Probably even an easy man to love."

His stare pierced into her, his hazel eyes serious and vibrating with flecks of deep brown. "I still am that man."

She stood up, needing to be nearer to his height when she said this to him, for his stare alone would be her undoing if she didn't fight it with every fiber of her being. "Maybe, but in-between then and now, you kidnapped me and ruined me, Silas. You never once—not once—stopped to ask me what truly happened. To ask me if I was involved in Miss Sanders's death. You would have had the truth from my tongue before any of this had happened."

"You're right."

She turned from him, her right arm curling about her stomach and she reached for her glass of wine, taking another sip before turning back to him. "So yes, you are still that man from Toften Hall. But you are also the man that didn't have the common decency to ask me if I was a murderer. Who believed I could do such a thing. So what am I supposed to say to all of this? How am I supposed to act?"

"This is me, attempting to forge a path forward with you, Georgina." He took two steps toward her, his voice heated with intention. "I want you. I think you realize that by the way I look at you. By the way I talk to you. By the way I have not been able to keep my lips and hands off of you, even when I thought I needed to hate you."

His words bounced around in her head, making her feel light-headed. Making her wish his hands were on her

at that very moment. Making her feel exactly as she did at
Yarstone when his tongue and fingers were deep inside her.

She fought to stay focused on him. Focused on what he
had done to her. What he had stolen from her.

Her shoulders pulled back as she steeled her spine.
"You must understand, in what has happened these last
weeks—what you have made happen—is that I have been
put on a ship that is sailing in only one direction and there
is no way to dive off of it. No land in sight, so I have to stay
on the ship because it is the only thing keeping me afloat."

He shrugged, his shoulder muscles straining against the
white lawn shirt. "Marriages have been forged on less."

"Love has not."

"That is what you truly want? Love?"

"Is it so silly that you cannot even imagine that is what
I want? My aunt and my uncle are the only parents I have
ever really known and I grew up watching how much they
adore each other. How much they love each other. Why
wouldn't I want that for myself?"

He nodded. "And I took that away from you?"

"The chance for it. Yes, you have."

"You are a dreamer, aren't you?" He sighed, his
eyebrows lifting. "Need I remind you, you were going
to elope with that bastard, Leroy, and live in a loveless
marriage."

"Except it wasn't going to be loveless." Her right hand
rubbed against her flat belly. "That child was my love. I
would have done anything…" She turned away from him,
not wanting to let tears fall in front of him again.

So many damn tears when she'd always been slow to cry. She'd been like this, crying at a pin drop for the last month, ever since she'd lost the babe.

He moved fully toward her and his hand went to her neck, burying into the thick of her hair hanging down her back until his fingers reached her skin. "What you have been through…I'm sorry." His voice dipped, low and thick in a way that wrapped around her chest and squeezed. "Sorry for my part in it. Sorry for what you have suffered beyond me. You didn't deserve any of it, but all that pain found you. And I played a role in that which I regret with every fiber of my being."

Genuine.

His words so genuine, all of her defenses crumbled about her as he wrapped his arms around her. She curled into him and he held her to his chest, her nose tucked into the crook along the center of his torso.

She let him. Let him hold her up rather than find footing of her own.

It was the first time since her family had arrived in London that she had felt safe. Felt that someone was watching over her so she didn't have to be on edge, one eye and one ear open at all times to protect both Willow and herself.

Silas gave her a space she could crawl into and not think. A space she desperately needed.

Moments passed and it became harder and harder to deny how his body was pressed against hers. How she could feel every muscle, every breath his body took. How her folds had started to flush with throbbing heat as the scent of him enveloped her.

The devil help her, it wasn't right.

None of this was right. He'd kidnapped her. Ruined her.

And yet she felt safe in his arms. So incredibly wrong, but her body was refusing what her brain was screaming.

She brushed her nose up slightly, then down along the V of his lawn shirt, staying hidden against his chest as she cleared her throat. "Tell me again how wrong you were."

His chest rumbled in a chuckle, his hand pressing harder into her neck, holding her against him. His face dropped down, his lips landing on the top of her head. "If I could erase the entire last six months for you, especially my part in it, I would do it in a heartbeat."

"But then I never would have met you."

"I would do it in a heartbeat. Do it to save you from all of the pain you have had to endure. Do it because you deserve only the good in the world, and the world has only served you bad."

"It hasn't been all bad."

"No?"

"That kiss we shared—that very first kiss at Toften Hall in the woods. That was magic." She smiled to herself as his body twitched at the mention of it, his shirt tickling her nose, his member hard and insistent and protruding into her belly. "It was gentle and true and heartwarming with the promise of all the things that could be discovered."

"It was that," he said, his lips not moving from the top of her head.

"And then the kiss we shared after you saved me from the whorehouse—that one was magic of a different sort. Wrong and raw and a force from the bowels of the earth that I couldn't deny and I didn't want to need, but I did. And what it turned into—that wasn't magic, that was just pure carnal lust. Neither of us wanted it, but our bodies demanded it, wrong as it was."

Her hands flattened, slipping along his sides, his muscles flexing at her touch. She lifted her head, finding his eyes. "What is this between us? Why is it so hard to deny when everything rational tells me it will destroy me?"

"It's already destroyed me." The heat in his eyes set fire to her veins. "I think I've just succumbed to dragging you down with me."

"Then why are we doing it?"

His hand lifted, the tips of his fingers wisping along her hairline from the center of her brow downward until he cupped the side of her face. "You're a dreamer, Georgina. But this between us—it isn't a dream. It's obsession. It's raw. It's gritty and demanding and needy. But wrong?" He shook his head. "I beg to differ."

She drew in a trembling breath. "And if it destroys me?"

"Then I will put you back together. Whole, so you can dream again." He dipped down, his lips brushing the side of her cheek, his voice a low rumble. "Do you want this?"

"Do you?"

A silent chuckle left his lips, his breath warming her ear. "I think it's pretty evident what I want. I want you.

I don't think I've made a secret of that since I pulled you from the side of the road."

She pulled away, searching his face, searching his eyes. Surrender.

As much as what he'd done to her in the last weeks screamed at her to resist, rational thought was useless. The unexplainable draw her body had to his was a force she couldn't battle.

This was where she fell firmly into the sin of surrender. The devil was here for her, and he'd come in the form of a man she was powerless to deny.

Her mouth opened, the tip of her tongue dragging across her top lip. "I know I shouldn't, but I do. I want this."

His mouth was on hers before she could take a breath.

His kiss a mix between the rabid frenzy of the kiss at Yarstone and the gentle, heated promise of the kiss at Toften.

Yet it was there in the kiss, pulsating under everything, that demanding need he had for her.

His tongue exploring, tasting, searching even as their breath melded. His hands moved along her backside, slowly, stripping her down.

Button by button. One arm free from the fabric, then the other. His shirt gone. Her shift slipping down her body. His fingertips grazing across her nipples, sending the peaks to attention, hardening under his soft touch. So soft, her body arched into him, wanting more, wanting hard, wanting everything all at once.

He wasn't about to rush it. His hands drifting along her body, sinking into the dips, trailing along the curves like it was a ride on a summer day and he had nowhere to be. His lips lazy along her neck, his tongue slipping out to taste her skin in the most sensitive spots.

As hard as it was to slow, she took the cues from him, tracing the lines of his body in heated silence. Pressing in along muscles that wouldn't yield to her touch, fingering scar after scar that dotted his skin on his chest and his arms.

For as handsome as he was, his body was a warrior's, through and through. Rigid, damaged, with muscles coiled to react. Every inch of him causing the spasms running through her folds to pulsate harder and harder and he hadn't even yet sent his hands below her waist.

His trousers dropped away and her breath stalled in her throat.

She hadn't expected—imagined this. His shaft tall and straining and so damn large. She had experience, yes, but only with Leroy and he was half the size of Silas.

As much as it sent a quiver of fear deep into her gut, her fingers reached out, needing to touch the smooth surface of his cock. Needing to feel the ridges, the steel of it. Needing to imagine it before she was actually presented with it.

He shuddered as her hand wrapped around the width of it, stroking upward.

"Hell, little dragon, I will not last long with caresses like that."

She smiled, her tongue slipping out to lick the middle of his chest, the small divot directly in the center. "Then you should move this along. I only need so much wooing."

He chuckled, low and fiery. "This wasn't about wooing you. It was about studying your body."

"Did you learn all you needed to?"

"We'll find out. I think I've found most of the most sensitive spots on your body, if the flush in your cheeks and the way your lips are pulsating red are any indication."

She nodded. "They are an indication." Her hands slipped up the front of his chest to wrap around his neck. "And I think I'm going to injure you soon if you don't make me feel all that you have been promising with those hands."

He smiled, leaning down and kissing her, catching her bottom lip between his teeth, his tongue running against the sensitive flesh as he lifted her off the floor.

Her legs wrapped around his waist and he set the tip of his member at her entrance. He let her lip pull away from his teeth. "Promises made are about to be promises kept."

His hands strong along her hips, he steadied her and then slammed up into her. A gasp racked her body, the first intrusion impaling her, shocking her body from toes to scalp. Too big. Far too big.

He lifted her, and the girth of him escaped her and she instantly needed it back, her body already greedy to fill the void he'd just made.

It shouldn't be that easy. It should be hard, slow, plodding along for the size of his shaft. But it wasn't. It was only need, pulsating deep inside of her, begging to have him filling her.

He set a rhythm, his grip along her body shifting her up and down, her thighs perched along his hips helping the leverage.

For as agonizingly slow as he'd removed her clothing, his cock driving into her was demanding and rabid. And set to the perfect angle to cause friction along her folds, yet still reach that spot deep within her that was life to a dying woman.

His shaft never wavered, desperate to bestow satisfaction while finding its own.

Her grip on him went frenzied, her nails digging into his shoulders, and he shifted her backward, setting her backside onto the edge of the table, clattering the dishes.

He leaned her back, his mouth diving to her right breast, pulling the nipple between his teeth and applying pressure, up until that fine line between pleasure and pain.

Her agonized scream told him exactly when he had reached it, and as he feasted on her nipples, he pulled his cock free, riding it up along her folds slowly, then pulling back and driving it deep into her sex. Hard. Alternating, again and again until her vision started to black out, her body strung to such a high pitch that she finally grabbed him around the waist, sinking her nails into him and not letting him pull out of her again.

She lifted herself up to balance against the length of him once more, riding him as he growled, his entire body straining as he took her in fiery chaos.

Until he drove hard up into her, collapsing and destroying everything she knew about what it was to be whole.

For she no longer was.

She was a thousand tiny fragments, no longer of her own body.

Yet she could still feel him, hear his agonized groan as he swelled deep inside of her, sending wet heat to the furthest recesses of her core.

Her body shaking with each wave of the orgasm, he held her up, held her against him.

Putting her destroyed body back together again, just as he promised he would.

{ CHAPTER 27 }

"I have a present for you."

Outside the front door of the coaching inn, Georgina eyed him, then the plump sack he carried in his left hand, suspicion thick in her eyes. "Do I want to know?"

He grinned at her, the air surrounding him feeling light for once in his life. And it had only taken emptying his seed into her greedy little body four times during the night to put what he guessed was true optimism for the future into his chest.

He wasn't quite sure, for he'd never felt it before.

He leaned down to her, his voice merriment. "Actually, I take that back. This is a gift for me, but it includes giving you something."

She smiled, her unique breathless chuckle at her lips. "A gift that isn't a gift—now I'm intrigued." She motioned to the burlap sack. "Do tell me what's in there."

He held the sack up in between them and opened it. She leaned over cautiously, as though she expected a snake to surge upward and strike her.

Her eyes lifted to him. "Melons?"

He nodded, the grin still playing on his lips. "Melons."

Her right eyebrow lifted. "We're bringing melons to Scotland?"

"No. This is only part of the gift." He cinched the top of the bag closed, holding it in his left hand, and reached into an inner pocket of his coat. He pulled out a dagger,

the blade clad in a thin leather sheath, and handed it to her. "This is the other part of the gift."

She didn't move to take the blade from him. "You're giving me melons and a knife?"

"Yes."

"I did not figure you for a gift bearer with such creativity."

"I imagine there will be a host of surprises about me in the future." He held the handle of the blade closer to her. "Take the dagger, Georgina. It's yours for one of the hidden pockets in that dress."

Her fingers wrapped around the black onyx handle of the blade. It was a simple blade, light, a dagger not made for show but for purpose.

She took it from him, holding it loosely between her forefinger and her thumb. He would have to correct that.

"Good. Now we're going to practice how you stab."

"How I stab? There is a right way to stab something?"

"There is if you want to do damage." He held up the bag of melons, swinging it back and forth. "And we're going to practice on these. You need to know how to stab something with flesh, so you know the feel of it, know how to twist the blade to cause pain. The melons will work for that."

She guffawed. "You want me to stab melons?"

He nodded.

Her look skittered about the street and the people passing. "Here? In the middle of the walkway? I can't do that."

"Why not?"

"People will look. People will think I'm strange."

He glanced around. No one was paying them any mind, but he also knew she didn't like people looking at her—if people were looking at her or Willow, it was because they were gossiping about her sister, ready to strike with a vicious comment.

Attention was to be avoided at all costs, if it was up to Georgina.

"Well, then, let us head back to the brook behind the stables." He held out his elbow to her and she slipped her hand into the crook of it. "The stable hand is readying our horses for the day, so it will save them from bringing the carriage around."

He led her down the lane between the coaching inn and the bakery next door to it. In short order, they were standing next to the gurgling water of a brook, and he had wedged one of the melons against two rocks for stability at waist height.

He glanced over at her. She was watching him with interest, but clear trepidation clouded her blue eyes. He pointed toward where she still awkwardly held the dagger. "Let's work on your grip, first."

He moved alongside her, lifting up her arm and clasping his fingers over hers as he adjusted the knife in her hand. "All fingers engaged, your grip should be secure, but loose. Too tight and it'll get knocked out of your hand the moment it hits something hard."

He stepped back. "Now stab the melon."

She looked at him like he was due for Bedlam, then stepped forward and gave a sweeping glance around her

with her mouth twisted to the side. With a quick breath, she stabbed the tip of the dagger into the side of the melon.

The tip barely breached the outer rind.

He held the melon and clasped his hand over hers on the dagger and yanked the tip of the blade free. "I know you're stronger than that. You've had me pinned to the bed more than once in the last twelve hours."

She laughed. "I feel silly."

"You won't feel silly if you ever have to actually sink a blade into someone. You'll just be grateful you practiced. You'll be confident. There is nothing more dangerous than an apprehensive person wielding a blade. So, please. Humor me."

She stared at him for a long breath, then nodded.

"Good." He stepped off to the side. "Now draw your elbow back, pick a spot on the melon and drive it in."

Georgina followed his instructions.

A perfect strike. Strong. The blade sinking to the hilt.

"Well done." He moved to hold the melon as she pulled the blade free. "Now we do it again and again and again until the melon is a sieve."

They worked on it for some time, Silas having her approach from different angles, with different holds on the blade and twisting as she drew it out, until she was laughing with glee every time the blade sank so deeply juice squirted into her face.

Juice he couldn't let just drip down her cheek.

After the last melon was mangled to pulp, he caught her around the waist and pulled her into him, his tongue slipping out to lick the melon juice off her cheek.

She laughed, squirming out of his hold. "Unless you are going to lick down every part of me, I need to wash all the stickiness of the melon off."

"Challenge accepted." He grabbed for her, but she danced away from his hands and went down to the edge of the water.

She rinsed off the dagger, wiping it clean on her skirt before setting it down on a rock next to her.

The sleeves of the deep violet traveling dress ended just below her elbows, and she splashed water up onto her forearms and then onto her face.

Droplets dripping from her chin, she stared over the rushing water at the dappled sunlight streaming down through the surrounding trees, a smile like she had just cracked the lock to the crown jewels on her lips.

How in the hell had he managed to capture her? She was a beauty. An ethereal being. Even more so without the constant worry in her eyes that had been permanent since he had first seen her.

Whatever he had done to make even the sharpest edge of that worry dull, it made him feel invincible to see her smiling, happy as she was in that moment.

He didn't want to interrupt her. He wanted her to stay next to the stream, in whatever feeling it was that was making her glow, so he moved to sit down next to her at the waterside.

Finding a nice round boulder as a seat, he folded his legs up, setting his forearms atop his knees, silent as she scrubbed away the sticky juice of the melon. Water splashed against the skirt of her dress, turning the deep violet hue so dark it looked black.

"Why did you ever let Leroy touch you?" The instant the words were out, he regretted them. He wasn't even sure where that question came from or why it left his lips without thought.

Both of her hands in the water stilled as she looked over to him. "Are you asking because you are jealous or are you asking because you cannot believe what a fool I was?"

His shoulders lifted. No backing out of the question now. "The former, I imagine. I've never experienced jealousy before, so I suppose this is it. That and curiosity."

She nodded to herself, then continued to scrub her forearms clean. "The truth? After the first months of being in London, I felt like a piece of meat—merely flesh to be inspected and judged. I was half expecting some gentlemen to open my mouth and inspect my teeth."

Silas chuckled.

"You laugh, but it is true. They call it a mart for a reason. But really, all of that was a pretense, as the only thing the lot of those gentlemen were staring at was my inheritance." She splashed more water onto her face. "But with Leroy, it was easy. My uncle had hired him when we got to London, because he knew the London streets well, whereas our usual driver did not. Leroy was someone new to me. And he worked hard to charm me because he wanted me—as a person—not my dowry. That was refreshing and it made me feel like a real human being again. We both knew nothing could ever come of our entanglement, so there was no pressure."

"Why do you think he didn't want more?"

"Oh, we both knew there would never be a future for us." She waved her hand in the air. "He was a coachman. So we knew it could never become something serious."

"What is wrong with a coachman?" Silas bristled. "I'll remind you that I was a stableboy for my entire life until I joined the Guardians."

She looked at him, her brow furrowed for a moment. "There is nothing at all wrong about that. It is honest work. It is merely a fact that my uncle would never have allowed me to marry Leroy. That was why there was no pressure—we could just enjoy each other's company."

"Yet you thought less of him."

"No." Her head shook. "Hear me when I say I am well aware that greatness can come from humble beginnings. That any man can rise high above his start in life."

He nodded, then looked to the water bubbling just beyond his feet. "Do you think your uncle will embrace me?"

She pulled her hands from the water, shaking them, then dabbling them dry on her skirts. The fabric had already been ruined by the splatters of melons, so she was no longer bothering to take great care with it.

Shifting her skirts under her, she sat next to him on an adjacent boulder, her hand slipping onto the top of his thigh. "I think my uncle will need some time to accept that our foray in the London marriage mart did not go as planned. He had such high hopes for us making excellent matches."

He stiffened, even as he tried to control it. "And he will not see me as an excellent match?"

Her lips pursed as she considered the question. "I think he will see you as the man that didn't play by the rules. This is exactly what we all hoped to avoid given our dowries—a madcap run to the border in a scandalous elopement." Her fingers slipped inward, dragging along the inner side of his thigh.

She kept doing that, and they were never going to get to Scotland.

"Given that, you are doing an honorable thing by marrying me and he knows full well what the alternatives are. He doesn't want those alternatives to happen—for Willow and me to become spinsters or for the family to die out in this generation. He wants a legacy for the future."

He leaned into her, his palm running along her stomach. "So long as I put babes in your belly, he will accept me?"

She chuckled. "Do that, and you will become his closest confidante. But even without that, I know that in time, he will understand that a man such as you is the exact match I needed."

Silas nodded, drawing in a long inhale. He sighed it out. "We need to leave."

"Why?" She reached over and plucked her new dagger from the rock. "I was just feeling comfortable with the melon stabbing. I was going to ask you to buy some more."

"No. I need to get you closer to Scotland." He pulled her into him, nuzzling her neck. "The stabbing can wait. My cock cannot."

She laughed.

But she didn't argue.

{ CHAPTER 28 }

After making their way up the isle via carriage, they'd continued north from Durham on horseback because of the muck on the northern roads leading into Scotland. It was that or risk getting the carriage stuck along the way and thankfully Georgina had been game for the horseback ride and was a skilled rider.

Riding which would have been a hell of a lot easier if he hadn't had running through his mind every moment of the past four nights when his cock was deep in her.

No matter what it had taken—his mouth, his hands, his shaft. He used any and all means necessary to make Georgina come on him again and again. To make her feel like he was the only person that could ever make her body writhe from one height to the next. Anything to produce her screams, her nails running down his back, and the soft breaths she would take afterward with drowsy mewls mixed in. He needed all of it, all of her.

Most importantly, he needed her to know he would do anything for her pleasure. An apology with every stroke, with every touch, with every kiss. Anything to erase from her mind what he'd done to her.

He didn't know if he'd been successful at it, and he was bloody scared to ask, but he held hope on the matter.

Not that any of the times he'd had her naked body under his hands in the last days had sated him. For all he wanted in that moment after a long morning of riding was

to lead the horses off trail and find a secluded tree to ram her up against.

He shifted on his saddle.

Bloody uncomfortable.

Thank the heavens it was midday and they were approaching the next town.

He looked to Georgina.

She sat a horse well, taking the strides with ease, her body moving with the horse instead of against it. It was clear she'd lived most of her life in the countryside.

He pointed forward. "This is where we'll stop to change out the horses and get some food and drink."

A necessary stop, though he had been dragging the trip out. If he had been pressing it, they would have been on horseback the last few days and in Scotland already, but he'd taken the route slowly, wanting this time with Georgina. Doing his best to woo her, to convince her this wasn't a mistake—that he wasn't what she thought he was.

He wanted her to *want* to marry him by the time they arrived in Scotland.

Not marry him because it was her only reasonable option.

They stopped at the stables in Morpeth to change out the horses, then went to the coaching inn down the road for a few potpies to fill their bellies for the last stretch of the day.

Walking back to the stables, their steps were slow, neither one of them in a hurry to continue on with the day. So much so, his chest felt light, just like the air around him had for the last few days—a foreign feeling he still wasn't accustomed to.

"Tell me of your fondest memory of being a stableboy." Georgina looked up at him, her gaze landing on him a little longer than necessary.

A test of a question, he knew. She was attempting to ascertain whether he had actually worked in stables.

Test away, little dragon.

He smiled. "You would like to hear of all the dung I used to muck from the barns? I can recount the endless hours of it for you."

She laughed. "No, I said fondest. Unless you enjoy mucking excrement? Maybe that's a part of your personality you have yet to reveal to me?"

His palms went up with a grin. "No revelations on that end." His hands dropped as they continued to walk. "Let me think…ah, yes."

"What is it? I can see how your eyes just lit up."

He nodded, looking down at her. "It was a foaling. One of the mares was having a difficult time—feet were coming but no nose—and our stablemaster, Roy, had both of his arms deep into the mother, trying to find the foal's head. I had the nose of the mare to calm her—her name was Haven and she was a beautiful horse. A creamy white with freckles of brown across her nose. She was my favorite in the stable because she always nosed me in the back of the neck when she saw me—needing attention, but it was a gentle nudge, not an insistent one. Anyway, her breathing had started to slow, more blood than foal emerging, and most would have given up long before that time. But just when we thought we were to lose both of them, Roy managed to twist the foal and it came out."

"Did it live?" Her voice had gone tiny and he instantly realized he should have chosen a different story—this one would be far too raw for her.

He quickly nodded. "It did. He came out a gorgeous mix of black and white. His little wobbly legs finding footing right away. There was a peculiar beauty in the moment of that birth. To see a tragedy turn into magic. And it was all because one man wasn't about to give up."

She drew in a deep breath, her lips pulling inward. "And the mare?"

"Lived and gave us three more foals after. A great dam by all accounts. She doted on those foals."

Georgina nodded. "That…that is a wonderful ending." She looked up at him, her eyes narrowing. "You aren't changing the story on my account, are you?"

"I am done lying to you, Georgina." He stopped, grabbing her hand and turning her toward him. "Yes, I have lied. But you need to know that everything I have said and done to you since I found you along the road walking away from Yarstone has been the truth. Nothing but it. And I never intend for that to change."

Her head tilted, her piercing blue eyes searching his face. "I like that you make an intention and not a promise to that effect."

His brow crinkled. "You do?"

"I will expect that someday you will lie to me when I'm wearing something atrocious, but I think I look beautiful. That is a good time to lie. Also about how I look in the morning after rolling around in your bed all night. Another good time to lie."

"That, I'll never have to lie about." He leaned down and kissed her, disregarding the fact they were in the middle of the street for all to see. "You are nothing but perfection in the morning. You are the real you, with mussed hair and bruised lips. I could sink into you in the morning and never leave if it were allowed."

She laughed. "A lie or a truth, I'll take it."

He pulled back, his look serious on her. "A truth."

She paused, the smallest smile quirking the right side of her lips.

It took him a long breath to break eye contact and turn toward the stables.

It was going to be a hellish rest of the ride to Coldstream across the border. Would it be terribly crass to get a room at that coaching inn in the middle of the day and keep her captive in the bed for a week? Or two?

Marry her, first.

Marry her, and then he could honorably keep her in bed for a fortnight. Or a month. A month sounding better.

Not letting go of her hand, he forced his feet to continue moving toward the public stables.

A distance in front of them, a man disappeared into the alleyway beside the right side of the barn. A man he recognized.

What in the hell?

His grip tightened around her hand, and dragging her, he barreled through the people in the walkway to the front of the stables. He found the stablemaster.

He shoved Georgina into the stablemaster's arms, forcing the man to drop the bridle he was carrying and catch Georgina so she didn't fall. "Stay here. Stay with him."

He pinned the stablemaster with a look that demanded compliance. "Anyone dares to come near her, you slice them through. You hear me?"

The man had enough good sense to cover his surprise and he glanced at Georgina, then looked to Silas. "Yes, sir."

Silas ran out of the front of the barn and rounded the corner to the alleyway.

He had his dagger drawn by the time he sprinted down the length of it.

There, to his right. The brute he'd smashed into the stone wall days ago when he was harassing Georgina. The ass still had a white linen bandage wrapped around his head, dried blood staining the white.

He'd assumed the two men were just two asses cornering Georgina for amusement. He'd assumed wrong. This was no coincidence.

At Silas's footsteps, the brute turned around to him.

The man was too late for any reaction.

Silas had him shoved up against the wall of the building next to the stables, his arm hard across the man's chest and his blade angled into the man's neck before the brute could run.

"Why in the hell are you following us?"

The man shook his head, his mouth pulling to a sneer and exposing the gaping holes from missing teeth. "Ye don't know what's comin' for ye."

Silas's blade pressed in and a thin line of blood leaked out onto the silver. "I've killed men for merely daring to look at me like you're looking at me now. I have no problem slicing your neck and letting you rot here." He shoved his forearm hard into the man's chest. "You want to live, tell me what you're doing following us."

"Slice me like ye sliced that man in the stables, will ye?"

"What?" Shock rolled through Silas and his grip on his blade loosened.

The brute laughed. "Ye didn't think anyone saw. I saw. I saw what ye did to that coachman in those fancy stables. Sliced him ear to ear, quick and clean."

A gasp hit his ears.

Georgina's gasp.

He looked to his right to find her standing at the end of the alleyway, her face horrified. Her blue eyes huge and cutting into him, her voice screeched, horrified and accusing. "What did you do?"

The brute kneed Silas in the gut, sending him just far enough backward that he could escape Silas's hold. The man took off running.

Years of instinct surged through Silas's body and sent his legs into motion to chase the brute, but he only made it two steps before he managed to still his feet.

Georgina was more important than catching that bastard.

He whipped around to her.

She was backing up, her hands clawing along the rough planks of wood on the outer wall of the stable, trying to disappear back into the alleyway.

Trying to run from him.

Again.

{ CHAPTER 29 }

Silas caught her before she'd even made it halfway down the alleyway.

She should have run.

Run as fast as she could.

Run a thousand times over from this man.

But her legs had turned into lead, every step weighing her down. Stopping her escape until Silas's footfalls thundered behind her and his arms landed on either side of her, boxing her in against the barn, his body pressing into her.

Locking her in place, his rapid breath heated the air between them.

He had too much breath. She had none.

"Stop," he hissed. "Just stop running from me at every damn turn, Georgina."

She looked up at him, horror rolling through her body and making her limbs shake, her voice in a roar. "Who? Who did you kill in fancy stables?"

He stared down at her, the hazel in his eyes throbbing a mess of dark colors. His mouth pulled tight, not willing to answer her.

She wedged her hands upward and pushed on his chest. "Who? Who did you kill?"

No answer.

She shoved at him again and again, her shoves turning into flailing fists that beat into his chest but made no impact.

He was a solid wall around her and he wasn't moving.

Hit after hit and he didn't flinch, didn't shift.

Silent until she fell back against the rough boards behind her, beaten down by her own powerlessness.

Her head clunked back against the wall and she stared at his face. "Who was it?"

"You know who it was." His voice low, deadly, holding back untold rage.

"Leroy."

He nodded.

Her head dropped forward, her hands reaching up to cover her eyes.

How had she been so stupid?

Of course he had killed Leroy. Of course.

"Who—who are you? I thought—I thought Lord Fugal and his cousins killed Leroy. Killed him because they knew we planned to elope. I thought…" The words gagged in her throat.

She had it in her mind long ago that Lord Fugal had killed Leroy, so that was what she believed. She'd never thought to challenge that truth. Not even when Silas had told her Leroy had claimed she was the one that killed Miss Sanders.

It had been so bloody obvious.

Silas exhaled a sigh, his breath heating the top of her head. "There is nothing I can say."

Her face whipped upward, her glare cutting him as her voice snarled. "You can say a lot of things."

He winced, pain flashing across his eyes. "Leroy—the man you had sex with—the man that sired that babe you carried. He. Touched. My. Wife. He killed her. *Killed her*. Reveled in it. He needed to be wiped from this earth. It had to happen and I was the one to make it happen. I make no apology for it."

The vehemence in his voice, the fury boiling under his words stole away all the rage from her chest.

He was right. Leroy wasn't the man she thought she knew. There was no defending him. There was no more sadness at his death, for he had killed Josie—killed Silas's wife. Wanted to kill their babe.

Silas's hand slammed against the board to the left of her head. "And dammit to hell, I would do the exact same thing to any man that dares to touch you."

She jumped, startled, and it took a moment to catch her breath, her chest lifting in a shaky inhale. For all the questions she should ask in that moment, only one word eked from her lips. "Why?"

His stare devoured her, ripping out her soul. "You know why."

"Do I?"

"I love you, Georgina. If I am honest, I fell in love with you the first day I met you. I fell in love with you a month before we even met when I watched you dress down Lord Flewman after he cut Willow at Almack's. You are fire. You have the soul of a dragon. And I would give up my life, my

body, everything I am and have for you. And an agonizing death unto the man that would dare harm you."

Stunned, she stared at his face, at his beautifully shaped lips, at his eyes that sank directly into her chest, and her mouth went dry, her tongue freezing. She had to remind herself to breathe. "You love me like you loved Josie?"

"No."

She gasped before she could hide it, the hurt in that one word splitting her in two. She turned, dipping down under his arm boxing her in to move away from him. She couldn't stand there and listen to how she was less than, for she already knew she was.

She was nothing compared to Josie. Josie knew what she was doing, every minute of every day. Knew how to get anything done. Knew how to protect herself and her and Willow. Knew how to just *be*.

She was nothing compared to Josie.

What in the world had possessed her to even ask that foolhardy question?

"Wait." Silas grabbed her arm, stopping her and stepping around her. His hands moved to not box her in again, but to land on her shoulders, his thumbs curling up onto her neck. "You need to understand, I love you in a way I never could love Josie. She…she was my best friend since I was eight and she was seven. She was my only solace in a world that was going to crush me. She was my hope when I had none. She had belief in me when I had none. She knew I would have a future when I didn't believe I'd live to see another day."

He paused, swallowing hard. "I loved Josie, yes. I would do anything to protect her and that's why I married her. But that love was much different than what I feel for you."

Her eyebrows drew together, confusion clouding her brain.

He stopped, swallowing hard. "Josie could never love me back in the way I needed. She wouldn't let me touch her. She wouldn't let anyone touch her."

"What?" Her head shook. "No. I touched her all the time. Our arms were often linked when we were walking about the streets. She was my dear friend, you realize."

He exhaled a long sigh. "She wouldn't let any *man* touch her."

"Oh." Georgina paused, letting that statement and all the possible atrocities it contained settle into her mind. "Not even you?"

He shook his head. "Her father had set her onto that path at a very early age. He took advances upon her and it didn't stop until he went to the colonies for several years to salvage his slave trading empire. The raw evil that runs through that man is unimaginable."

She gasped, her hand over her mouth.

"I know. I would never speak of it, never speak of what happened to Josie, but you need to know how it was. Josie could never stomach a man's touch. Never. And when we found out her father was coming back to England, I convinced her to marry me. It was the only way we could keep her out of his clutches. She was his property, and he would have just started back up abusing her."

Georgina's stomach roiled, the thought of all her friend had suffered making her close to retching. Her hand flew over her mouth and it wasn't until her stomach stopped convulsing that she could look up at him. "I never…I never knew."

"You wouldn't. She didn't tell anyone. Ever. I only knew because I saw it once, what he was doing to her, and then I made her tell me."

"So you saved her from him."

"I did. I loved Josie. But I loved her like a sister. I had to. It was all it could ever be."

Her hands lifted, settling on his chest, feeling the strum of his heartbeat under her fingertips. "You married her knowing you could never have a family, a real future together?"

"I would have done anything to protect her. Marrying her was an easy choice."

She nodded, so much of what had happened during the past month now making sense. "And marrying me?"

"Was not an easy choice."

Her hands fell away from his chest, her eyes closing as her head dropped.

His thumbs shifted upward under her chin, lifting her look to him. "It was not an easy choice because you… you I knew I could love fully. You I knew could destroy me, through and through." He paused, closing his eyes for a long breath. He opened his eyes, his look sinking into her. "So no, I did not come about it lightly. I came about it with the weight of the world and a lifetime attached to it. A world and a lifetime I want with you."

She exhaled, his words dropping into her gut to warm her, yet all of it was too much. This, right after she discovered he'd killed Leroy.

He was a killer and openly admitted it to her.

Too much.

She grabbed his wrists, pulling his hold away from her neck, her voice a whisper. "I need to think—think away from you."

His hands drifted away from her and he let her step away.

Let her walk to the end of the alleyway and into the stable where she mounted her waiting horse.

He let her, but she knew he was five steps behind her.

She wasn't sure whether that was a good thing or not.

{ CHAPTER 30 }

Georgina had set her horse back from his.

Distance enough where they couldn't talk, but he was still within yelling and protecting distance. Every time Silas glanced back to her, her head was bowed, her stare solidly on the ground in front of her horse, the lines along her brow furrowed in thought.

He didn't push her and tried not to expect anything from her, even if it was deuced hard not to.

He'd killed her lover.

So she needed time to dwell on that.

He tried to understand, even though all he wanted to do was drag her off her horse and shake her to get answers out of her. To find out if it was the killing part or the killing her lover part that had her so taken aback.

They were still headed north, though. She hadn't balked at the direction, so he'd taken solace in that. And she'd had ample time to dwell on heading south instead of north while he had scoured the town to find that bastard that had gotten away from him. But the man had disappeared.

He needed to get Georgina to Coldstream, as it would be the safest place in the area for her, before he went after the blackguard.

They had travelled fast, pushing the horses. But she also hadn't spoken a single word to him since they left Morpeth.

Three hours after they had set out, he directed his horse down through an opening in the forest that led to a stream. After glancing behind him to make sure Georgina had followed him, he dismounted and led his horse to the edge of the stream for water.

As his horse drank, he pulled a wineskin from one of the saddlebags.

Her horse moved next to him and Georgina pulled up on her reins. He walked around the mare and grabbed Georgina by the waist, lifting her down before she could jump down on her own.

Really, he just wanted her body next to his. To feel in her muscles what her reaction to him was. Tense or not. Malleable or not. Furious or not.

That was just one thing he liked about Georgina. She was a disaster at hiding her emotions. He usually knew by her face what she was thinking, and if not by her face, he could read it in the rigidness of her muscles.

By the time her feet were on the ground, he had an inkling of what was moving through her mind.

She wasn't furious. She was confused. Thoroughly confused and on edge because of it.

She glanced up at him, somewhat awkwardly with a small smile. "Thank you."

He nodded.

She quickly twisted out of his hold and grabbed her horse's bridle and led it the last few steps to the stream.

Leaving the horses to drink and munch on the grassy slope by the stream, she shuffled backwards up the bank, and then stopped, her stare staying on the water.

Silas moved to stand next to her, facing the stream as well. He braved a glance toward her. "Have you done all the thinking you needed to?"

She nodded. "I think I could mull this over from here till kingdom come."

He pulled the stopper on the wineskin and handed it to her. "But you are not?"

"No." She took a sip of the wine, then handed him back the wineskin.

He took a drink, then pushed the stopper back in place, bent to set it on the ground, then straightened. "So?"

She exhaled a sigh, seeming to brace herself. "I don't want this."

He turned fully toward her, his chest tightening. He would give her all the space she wanted, except no—not if this was where she ended up. "You don't want to marry me?"

She glanced up at him as her arms wrapped around her middle. "No."

A snake of panic twisted about his gut.

Calm. Calm. *Calm.*

"Why not?" His voice was screaming in his head, but he forced his words to come out halfway stoic.

She turned to face him. "Because you are attempting to right your mistake in kidnapping me. The offer of marriage is honorable and I appreciate the gesture, but that is not what I want to be the rest of my life. A mistake. A mistake that needed fixing. For me to marry you is cowardly."

The screams in his head quieted. Marginally. "Have you heard anything I've said? That I want you? That I love you?"

Her mouth pulled back to the side, her gaze flickering off of him. "I hear you say that, but I cannot believe it. I cannot trust it. Not after…"

Trust. He was asking her to trust him when she had no reason to do so.

"Fine. Then we don't start there. We don't start with love. We start with what I did. Should I have stolen you away? No. Should I have asked you what happened and actually listened to the answer? Absolutely. A thousand times over on each account. All of that happened and yes, it was a mistake on my part."

He stepped closer to her, closing the distance between them. "But *you* are not a mistake." He started to reach out to her for he needed nothing more than the feel of her skin under his palms. But he held his hands steady at his sides, attempting to not scare her away when she was already teetering on the edge of leaving him. "You are the opposite of a mistake. You are my salvation. My fire. My obsession. My breath. But a mistake? No. Never."

Dammit—to hell with keeping his hands off of her.

He stepped in, sliding his fingers in along her jawline until he was cupping her face and could feel her blood pulsating under his fingertips. "The only one holding a mistake is me in how I treated you. I am the mistake. Not you. Not what we could be together. But if that is what this is really about—that you cannot forgive me for kidnapping you—then tell me. Tell me honestly and tell me now and we will turn around and I will bring you to London and leave you alone forever. I understand that is exactly what I deserve. There is no excuse for what I did, no matter how out of my mind I was when Leroy told me you demanded he kill Josie."

She flinched. "I never—"

"I know. I know you didn't. I know it was a lie. But at that time, when he told me that, everything twisted in my mind. Everything that I felt for you up until that moment distorted into the exact opposite."

Her cheeks lifted, pained. "Hate?"

He nodded, his breath heaving in his chest. "So much blasted hate. So much it was all I could see, all I could think. And if I only have one regret in my life, that was it. Believing that bastard's lie for even a second." He seethed in a breath, his head shaking. "But you need to tell me now, Georgina, if you cannot forgive me. I will bring you back to London. But I need to do it now before I cannot."

Her eyes went wide, her lips parting in a shallow breath. "You would really do that? Bring me home?"

His fingers lifted alongside her face, clutching her. "I would do anything for you. Anything for you to find peace. To find the future that you want. That you deserve. It may kill me, but if you have that—a future, peace—then I will accept it. I will accept it because that is what you wanted. What you chose."

"And if I choose to continue north with you?"

"Then you have me. Body and soul. For the rest of our lives." His head dropped, hating himself for what he had to ask next. His eyes lifted to her. "Unless you cannot live with what I am, what I do. The blood on my hands. The blood that will always be on my hands."

She drew in a trembling breath and he stilled, waiting for his fate to rise from the ashes of the scorched earth of his past.

Her blue eyes scoured his face, her lips pulling inward for a second before parting. A breath. Two.

She gave the tiniest nod to herself, her cheeks brushing under his palms, her stare landing on his. "Horrible choices are made in life, forced upon us when we are not ready for them, and we do what we need to in order to survive. I cannot condemn you for any of the choices you've had to make. Except, for the kidnapping me part—that part I am still wrestling with. I know I should hate you for it—I do hate you for it—but it isn't all I feel. And the feeling part… the feeling part is so much more, whether I want it to be or not. I cannot control it."

The very soul of him clenched, his body still, desperate for her next words.

Her right hand lifted, her fingertips following his brow just along his hairline before her palm flattened against his cheek. The wisp of an angel. "Whatever made you, whatever forged you into the man you are now, standing in front of me, I want him. All of him. Past and present and future. Mistakes and all."

She damn well stole his breath. Grace he didn't deserve.

But the lack of air in his lungs couldn't stop him from descending on her, his lips meeting hers in a rabid frenzy.

She met him with all the angst, all the indecision raging through her. Indecision he was going to banish from her head.

His lips bruising hers, he picked her up, slipping his hands under her thighs as she wrapped her legs around him. Five steps away from the bank of the stream and he had her back propped against a tree.

Her hands went down, frantic between them as she freed the fall front of his trousers. His cock hit the air and he couldn't drag her skirts up her thighs fast enough.

His shaft, furious and raging that it wasn't already deep inside of her, strained painfully as her fingers wrapped around the length of him. She stroked him full, her fingers slipping down to massage his balls, then drifted up again, grabbing his cock with force.

Heaven to hell, how had this goddess fallen into his life?

Her skirts high and out of the way, he reached inward, swiping along her slit. Drenched. Ready for him.

He broke the kiss, pulling away from her, his stare locking into her eyes. Her blue irises shining like glass forged from the early morning sky, begging to be shattered.

He lifted her a touch higher and set the tip of his shaft at her entrance, his look not wavering from her face.

He loved watching this moment play out on her features—the moment he drove his cock into her and her eyes lit up, her composure wrecked—an ethereal beauty breaking apart piece by piece.

His own composure near to fracturing, he slammed up into her in one thrust and the most beautiful grunt vibrated up from her chest. Guttural and raw.

That was exactly how he needed to take her in this moment.

Carnal and savage and possessive, just like nature intended.

She'd given him permission, given herself to him, and now he needed to mark her, erase any last doubt in her mind that she was his.

That one thought pounded in his head with each thrust, with each groan she uttered into the forest air. She was his. Finally. His.

She finally understood what he had known from the first moment he saw her. She was his.

Her fingertips ripped into his neck as her right hand went above her head, gripping the tree, holding her body at the best angle to grind against him.

His breath gasping with every drive into her, again and again, her groans flipped into screams and within a minute, she shattered against him.

His balls tightened as her inner walls went greedy, locking onto him, and he came, erupting into her, her violent contractions forcing every last drop of him deep into her body.

He collapsed against her, crushing her to the tree, crushing her against him. Fighting for breath. Fighting for sanity when it was nowhere to be found.

She was dangerous to him without even knowing it— he'd known that from the first.

Yet it wasn't until that moment that he realized the danger of her tearing him apart was long past.

She'd already done so.

And he wouldn't have it any other way.

{ CHAPTER 31 }

"How did you and Josie become best friends when you were eight and she was seven?"

Silas's eyes lit up, a sliver of a smile curving his lips. It was clear every time he talked about Josie how much he respected her—loved her. Something she would have to wrestle with, for as much as she had adored Josie, it was hard to not compare herself with the ghost of her friend.

He looked down at her as they walked along the bustling main road of Coldstream. They had already deposited the horses at the stable behind the coaching inn they would be staying in that night after finding the man that would still marry them today.

"It was on a summer day. Hot. It was oddly hot that day, I remember. Everyone was sweating, even in the shade. I was a stableboy at her father's estate just outside of London proper. I was getting whipped—the stablemaster loved his riding crops."

The smile still stayed on his lips, weirdly juxtaposed to the memory of being whipped.

Her gut twisted. "Whipped—whatever for?"

He shrugged. "One didn't need to do much to make Ole Roy angry. I was small then and he hated small, weak things. I probably sloshed some water out of a bucket or missed cleaning up some crap in the corner of a stall."

"How awful." Her face twisted, already hating this story and the random stablemaster from long ago.

"It was what I expected daily in those days. I was an orphan, just doing anything I could for food to eat and a place to sleep."

"Wait." She grabbed his forearm. "You were an orphan? What happened to your parents?"

He shrugged. "I never remember having a mother. A father, I have vague snippets of in my memory. A man with ruddy red eyes and tufts of hair scattered about his head. And one day, that man was just gone. I don't remember much of how I ended up at the stables, only that I was there and that was where my first real memories started."

It took her a moment to settle all of that into her head. Josie had done wonders for opening her eyes to the harsh realities of the people of London—more so than anything she'd witnessed before. But Silas being an orphan—a beaten orphan—was hard to digest and even harder to imagine without tears flooding her eyes.

Not that he would want her pity. But it didn't stop her heart from cracking at the thought of him as a child.

She schooled her features. "So you were being whi—whipped." She stuttered out the word, caustic as it was to her tongue.

"I was. And Josie—little seven-year-old-Josie with her brown hair in pigtails and fat curls came into the stables. She saw what was happening and screamed and told Ole Roy to stop. He laughed at her and kept whipping me." He looked up at the sky, his head shaking. "That was one thing you didn't do to Josie—laugh at her. The next thing I knew, she dove in front of me, right in front of the leather crop he was beating me with."

She gasped. "Did she get hit?"

"She did." He looked down at her. "On purpose."

"What?"

His finger motioned along the edge of his face. "That scar along her cheekbone, right by her hairline."

Georgina nodded. She remembered it well. It was a faint white line—old—but it was there.

"It was exactly what she wanted to happen. She ran off, bloody, to tell her father what Ole Roy had done to her. He was immediately beaten to within a breath of life by her father's men and then driven out of the area—probably out of all of London." The smile hadn't left his face as he shook his head. "Even at that age, Josie knew where the power was. And how to manipulate that power."

Georgina remembered that about her friend. Josie knew how to take men down, how to threaten them until they were quaking in their boots. There were countless wastrels in London that Josie had thrown off from hunting after her and Willow during the season. "She was a force. I never knew how much so."

"That she was." He nodded, the memory still warming his eyes. "The next week we got Mr. Poppet as our stablemaster. And Mr. Poppet was always more than good to me. He taught me not only about horses and life on the streets of London, but how to fight as well. While Josie taught me how to read and write and about mathematics because she needed a friend. Her father kept her in a tiny cage—he wouldn't let her out of the house and gardens, so she had no other contact with people aside from the staff, and I was the only one close to her age. I became her friend by default. She taught me how to think, and I taught her how to fight and about London once her father left for the colonies and she got a taste of freedom."

"How did she become a guardian? She never told us." Georgina frowned as she waved her hand up and down his body. "Quite clearly, she never told us much about her life."

"Once she had that freedom to disappear into London at night without her guardian knowing, she wanted more—so much more—but mostly she wanted to hurt evil men. She would go out without me sometimes, even though I would yell at her for doing so. But she had so much rage in her back then, and one night, one of the guardians found her stabbing a man that had been raping a girl in an alleyway. He thought she would make a fine recruit, but she would only do it if I became a guardian as well."

"How old were you then?"

"I was sixteen, she was fifteen. It changed my life, again. I thought I was destined to be a stablemaster just like Mr. Poppet. But then the Guardians happened. The title happened."

"She brought you everything you ever needed."

He nodded, then paused his steps. "She did. Everything I never thought to aspire to. She even brought me to you. And you are what I always needed in my life, but I never would have recognized it myself. You are where the rest of my life belongs."

Staring up at him, with the heat in his eyes that never seemed to dull when he looked at her, her lips parted as a trembling breath sank into her lungs.

The rest of his life. The rest of *her* life.

She couldn't even put into rational thought how much she wanted this. Wanted this with him.

Once she had let herself believe it—truly believe that she could rise from the ashes of what her life had become, she wanted a future with Silas more and more with each passing second. "Tell me that this is real. What I want. What I feel."

His face sobered as his hand lifted, his finger dragging along the side of her face. "If it is even a tenth of what I feel for you, how I want you, then yes, it's real. Make no mistake. It is real."

He grabbed her hand, tucking it into his elbow, and he started down the walkway once more. "Can I ask a favor of you?" He squeezed her tucked hand after a few steps.

She pulled her gaze away from the window of the milliner's shop adjacent to the walkway to look at him. "Yes?"

He pointed to the front window of the next building. "Will you go into this shop and get a new dress and hat?"

She had thought they were walking directly to the blacksmith's shop that the innkeeper had pointed them to. Apparently, the man there wasn't even a blacksmith—there were just so many couples coming through this town to elope, that the man had bought a vacated blacksmith shop and turned it into a space that only performed weddings.

Georgina looked at the ready-made dresses hanging in the dressmaker's window he pointed to and her free hand unconsciously smoothed down the front of the violet dress she had chosen from Josie's wardrobe. "Why? Am I

not appropriate? I realize that this is a traveling dress, but I cannot imagine the man doing the ceremony will care."

Silas stopped, his hazel eyes serious as he turned toward her and slid his hands in along her waist. "You are beautiful just as you are. But I want to marry you, all of you, down to whatever you choose to wear—not something that was available. Not something that holds the ghost of the one before you."

She looked past his shoulder at the dress shop, a pang singeing across her chest. Her heart both breaking and swelling at the same time.

He had loved Josie dearly and she would never disparage him for that, though the pain he was in because of her death nearly undid Georgina.

Yet even with that pain, he wanted her—wanted who she was down to her bones. Down to the clothes she wore. He wanted *her*.

She nodded, her voice catching. "I can do that."

"Good." The smile went easy onto his face. "Then I also want to be surprised by what you pick."

"Surprised? You do?"

"I don't get a lot of surprises in life. My job is to know everything all of the time. So this one would be nice."

The grin on her face went ridiculously wide. She didn't care. This was a spark of innocence in Silas she never would have expected and it pleased her to no end.

He reached into an inner pocket of his coat and then pressed a sizable purse of coins into her hands. "Whatever you want, I know I will adore it." He leaned in, his breath tickling her neck as his voice dipped into a low whisper. "Or I'll at least adore stripping it off of you in a few hours."

She laughed, pushing at his chest before he convinced her to turn around to the coaching inn and never make it to the blacksmith's shop. "I will be sure to choose a dress with the least arduous buttons for you to pop free."

"See that you do." He inclined his head down the street. "I am going to go down the lane to see if there is another shop that I would like to visit before the ceremony."

Curiosity lifted her eyebrows. "Oh? What shop is that?"

"Better you don't know so you can be surprised as well."

She giggled and waved her hand. "Go on. Let us get this done so we can make our way to the blacksmith that is not a blacksmith."

He stepped past her and opened the door to the dress shop. "Don't leave the shop until I get back." He paused, taking his standard predatory scan around the street at the horses and carts and coaches rolling past. "Stay in the shop—promise me."

"I will stay in there and spend money until you return. How is that?"

He chuckled, his look landing on her. "Well played, my soon-to-be-wife."

Georgina stepped into the shop and was immediately greeted by a shopgirl. Together they went through the many options of ready-made dresses that would fit her, and she tried on three of the dresses before settling on a beautiful, simple pale peach silk dress that fell in an elegant sweeping fashion from the waist. Silver trim edged the waist, hem and

bodice, with sheer short sleeves. Completely impractical for anything other than a summer house party or dinner—or a wedding. Even more impractical for the cool air prevalent in this area of the isle.

She stood in front of the mirror, her stomach a nest of buzzing bees as the shopgirl buttoned up the back of the dress. Not as easy an escape as she had promised Silas, but she also knew he wasn't above popping a few buttons to get at her body.

"Oh. One thing. I need a hidden pocket for this dagger." She went to Josie's violet travelling dress and ruffled through the fabric until she found the hidden pocket at mid-thigh on the skirt and she pulled free the blade Silas had given her. She'd promised him she'd keep it on her at all times, and she wasn't about to start off their marriage with a broken promise.

The shopgirl's eyebrows lifted in part curiosity and part disapproval, but then she nodded. "Of course." She hurried off to find a needle and matching thread.

It took a bit of extra time for the shopgirl to split the seam and sew in a pocket the exact size and length of the dagger, but when it was done, Georgina liked how the opening to the pocket blended into the cut of the pale skirt.

Finished, the shopgirl wrapped up Josie's violet dress in a satchel, as Georgina knew she would need it for the journey back to London.

The shopgirl went next door and returned with a new hat—small, silver and jaunty that completed Georgina's outfit. She still wore the boots she'd been travelling in, but they would be fine. It wasn't worth buying a new pair of slippers for a few hours.

As much as she'd like to spend all of the coins Silas had given her, she'd been raised to be practical by her aunt and uncle.

The whole of it took much longer than she had anticipated and she was surprised Silas hadn't already returned to impatiently tap his foot at the door.

She waited. Waited longer.

Waited with awkward glances, weak smiles and mindless talk with the shopgirl until dusk had started to dim the sky.

It had been far too long, no matter how many shops he had needed to visit. Two hours, maybe more. And the shopgirl was on edge, clearly wanting to close for the evening.

Georgina thanked the girl again and stepped out into the evening air. A chill had descended as the sun had lowered in the sky and goosebumps spread onto the back of her bare arms. She was suddenly regretting her choice in dresses. She had thought it would be crumpled to the floor in their room at the coaching inn by now.

Trepidation spun in her belly as she looked down the street where she had last seen Silas. Much of the traffic from the day had disappeared, only a few wagons rolling along the street.

She looked both directions. No Silas.

Her heart started to thud hard in her chest.

He'd abandoned her.

Abandoned her in Scotland—as far from home as possible.

The vicious cruelty of it. He'd been playing the long ruse. Looking to own her—body and soul—only so that he could leave her in the middle of some random town on the opposite end of the isle.

She staggered back a step, leaning against the door of the dress shop as all feeling left her limbs, her head going light.

He'd *abandoned* her.

The door suddenly moved to open behind her and she jumped a step away.

"Oh, my apologies, miss. Did you forget something in the shop? Or need anything else?" The girl gave her a kind smile, but fidgeted, clearly ready to leave for elsewhere.

"No." Georgina forced a bright smile on her face. "I was just enjoying the evening air for a moment before moving on my way."

The shopgirl nodded. "Good eve, then." She stepped past Georgina and moved off down the street.

Georgina watched her go, envious of the young woman. She had somewhere to be. Someone was waiting for her.

She swallowed down the panic that was bubbling up from her churning stomach and turning into hard rocks that lodged in her throat.

Silas had left her.

Except no.

She had felt it. *Felt it.*

She was a dreamer—always had been—and it had gotten her into trouble more times than she could count.

For once, she had to listen to her brain. Had to accept the fact that he was gone. Had to accept the fact that she was wrong—always wrong.

Except that she had felt it.

She had felt in her marrow, how much he loved her.

She was a dreamer and there wasn't anything for it.

So she would listen to her heart. For she would always and forever make the same mistake of leading with her heart, over and over again, because it was who she was.

She would chase love.

Hope for it. Fight for it.

Even if it crushed her.

{ CHAPTER 32 }

She started down the street, following in Silas's footsteps from earlier.

First shop, closed. Next one, closed. Three shops down she finally found a bookstore that was open. Yanking the door open, she dashed in and startled an elderly bespectacled man reading a book behind a counter.

"Has there been a man in here recently?" She rushed forth, the parcel holding Josie's dress swinging from her wrist as she slapped her hands on the counter. "Dark hair, hazel eyes? About this tall?" Her hand flew up at her side. "Strong and with a look in his eye that defied one to antagonize him?"

Above the spectacles balancing on his nose, the shopkeeper's brow furrowed into a hundred tiny lines and he shook his head. "Nay, lass. None today. Only the Peterson sisters and their aunt since noon."

"Thank you." She rushed out of the shop, moving onto the next one.

A goldsmith.

Her gut sank as she looked through the small window at rubies glinting in the last rays of the sun in the sky.

Silas was going to the goldsmith. He had to have been.

A goldsmith shop that was now closed. Still, she grabbed the handle of the door, yanking on it just in case the darkness inside wasn't an indicator. The door didn't budge.

Frantic, she rushed into the tailor's shop next door. Neither of the men inside had seen Silas.

A sundry store. Nothing.

Hell, even a tiny toy shop. Nothing.

Beyond the toy shop at the end of the street, the buildings turned into houses.

A few people were still strolling along the walkway. Yet no Silas.

Blast. Was she making an even bigger fool of herself?

Was he watching from some hidden part of the street, chuckling to himself at her desperation?

She shook her head.

No.

No. He wouldn't leave her.

She looked across the street. A tavern.

She charged across the muck of the roadway, grateful she had kept her boots on as she stepped into something squishy and a pungent odor instantly assaulted her nostrils.

Wiping off her heel as much as she could in the next few steps, she stormed into the tavern, ignoring all the heads that instantly turned her way. She charged straight toward the barkeep. "Please, sir, I am looking for a man."

"There be plenty of those in here, lass." He swished a rag in the air toward the tables filled with men.

She reached out and grabbed his arm, slamming it down onto the top of the bar. "No. I'm looking for a specific man. He's tall and he has dark hair and hazel eyes and he is quite good at crushing anyone who crosses him. His clothes—they are fine—his tailcoat and his waistcoat are black with thin threads of blue running up and down. He's not from the area."

Recognition flickered in the man's eyes, but then he dropped his look downward to her hand still pressing down on his arm.

She snapped her hand away. "You know who I'm talking about—you saw him, didn't you?"

"I would think if ye came in here wanting answers, ye wouldn't be a harpy screeching demands like ye are. Ye'd be asking polite, an English lass like yerself."

She threw the entire purse of coins that Silas had given her onto the bartop. "Is this polite enough for you?" She leaned over the bar, her voice in a growl. "Tell me everything you know."

{ CHAPTER 33 }

"Where is she?"

Smack.

The fist of the brute with the missing front teeth and the gash Silas gave him days ago on his forehead slammed across his face.

Silas blinked, stars flickering in and out of his already cloudy vision.

Awake. Stay awake.

He couldn't afford blackness again.

Not like the minutes—or hours—ago when he had been coming out of the goldsmith's shop and a man had run into him, shoving him into the adjoining alleyway and directly into the other brute who grabbed his head from behind and slammed it into the brick wall.

Darkness had instantly descended.

Darkness when he was usually so adept at taking blows yet managing to keep his wits about him.

Not this time.

Not this time because he'd been vulnerable, walking out with his thumb running a circle along the edge of the ring in his pocket he'd just bought for Georgina. A ring he was envisioning slipping onto her finger as her face lit up and that distinct breathless laughter she possessed left her lips. Laughter that he'd only heard from her when she was with him. Laughter that told him, despite all odds, he was her happiness.

Damn rainbows and butterflies of the future had been in his eyes instead of what had been right in front of him.

The very thing that would crush his future.

He blinked again. Orientating himself after that last blow to his temple.

They were in a hayloft. The smell he knew well from his youth was thick in his nostrils. His arms were strung up high over his head, tied together with a rope that was attached to a pulley hanging from a rafter. Truthfully, the rope was the only thing holding him upright after that last punch shook his brain. Not that he even had the opportunity to get his feet under him, as only the tips of his toes touched the dusty, hay-strewn boards.

Three brutes now surrounded him. The toothless one reared back for another blow. Next to him was the flat-faced man he'd been with days ago. And now there was a third man, dressed better, standing out of the blood spray area. Just beyond the third man, the end of the rope was tied to a metal hook attached to the wall of the barn under the rafters.

Silas shifted his hands, testing the tightness of the knots around his wrists. Tight.

The fist came flying at him again, and this time, Silas was ready, moving with the blow. If one couldn't avoid the impact, the best thing to do was lessen it. The brute still got the satisfaction of fist meeting flesh, but Silas could keep his wits about him.

"I said, where is she?" The well-dressed man repeated himself, the disgusted glare on his face eating into Silas.

Silas stared back at him, buying time.

They were here for Georgina.

And the fact of the matter was, he would never give Georgina up. Death first. That was the only way he viewed it.

How long had he been out for? Hours? It'd been more than mere minutes for them to drag him up here and tie him up. The light coming into the stable had waned, dusk arriving. Where would she be right now? Still in the dress shop? Back at the coaching inn? Heaven forbid, looking for him.

He forced his cracked jaw that had been slack to close, his glare meeting the well-dressed man. Silent.

The man stepped toward him, a sneer pulling back on his lips. "Listen, you dung heap. You're going down, one way or another. We know you killed that man in the stables. That alone will get you the noose. This is us making sure she is taken care. So where is she?"

This was where he played dumb. "What are you talking about? Where is who?"

"Lady Jocelyn. Where is she?"

Lady Jocelyn? Silas had to shake his head to make sure he was hearing correctly. "Who?"

"Lady Jocelyn." The man nodded to the toothless brute and he sent another blow across his chin. "Where is she?"

He'd heard correctly. And if that was the case, then these men...

His chest heaved in a sigh.

These men had been sent by Josie's bastard of a father. He had never found Josie once he returned to England years ago.

And none of them had any clue she was dead.

How would they? He and Josie had become masters of hiding in plain sight within the system of power and prestige in London. But one would have to have known them when they were young to know where they came from.

No one did.

Except somehow, Josie's father had found out who he was. He knew who Silas was—how he had become Lord Atwell—and these brutes had been shadowing him for weeks. Maybe even months.

Bloody fucking hell.

If they had been shadowing him, then they sure as hell knew he'd been travelling all this way with Georgina.

Silas coughed, spitting out a wad of blood that had collected on his tongue. "I don't know what you're talking about."

"No?" The well-dressed man wandered past Silas strung up in the middle of the hayloft to the window just behind him letting the last vestiges of daylight in. "Well, if you cannot miraculously remember, then I will be forced to go down below and gut that pretty little bird walking along the street right now, looking for you."

Shit. No.

Silas twisted, trying to crane his neck to see over his shoulder. He could only see as far as the well-dressed man so his lips pulled back in a snarl. "There is no pretty bird down there looking for me."

The man chuckled. "No, there is." He bent over, glancing out the low window again. "Blond hair with streaks of red. Face of an angel. Skin so perfect and ready to be marked. She looks quite frantic."

His roar was immediate, his body twisting against the ropes stringing him up. "You touch anyone because of this and I'll flay you alive, you rat fucking bastard. I'll rip the skin from your flesh and shove it down your throat until you're gagging your way to hell on your own miserable blood."

The man snickered, knowing he had Silas just where he wanted him.

That was when Silas heard it, just under the grating sound of the man's laughter, a squeak. Another one.

Someone was climbing the ladder into the hayloft.

Shit. If it was Georgina, he was going to strangle her for being so stupid.

Josie—Josie he would have no trouble with her coming up to save him. But she'd been trained—properly—and knew how to take care of herself.

He hadn't had any time to train Georgina on anything. Not how to defend herself, and certainly not how to save someone in dire straits.

No time.

Because he'd wasted so damn much of it hating her when she didn't deserve it.

The only thing he could do now was draw attention away from the opening in the floor where the ladder led upward.

He lifted his right leg, twisting his hanging body as he swung his boot out at the toothless brute next to him. The motion stretched his left shoulder to pain until it popped.

One dislocated shoulder.

Worth it for the satisfaction of his heel catching the man directly in the kidney, sending him doubling over, howling.

The flat-faced brute and the well-dressed man stepped toward him. "You'll pay for that."

The flat-faced brute advanced on him, fists high.

"Wait. Wait." Silas heaved a dramatic breath. "I know where she is. I know where Josie is."

All eyes on him, he sucked in what sounded like a painful hiss, using the moment to glance to his right.

A head popped up through the cutout of the floor.

A red-blond head with the prettiest little silver hat atop her head.

Dammit all to hell.

Georgina's eyes went wide as she saw him strung up and about to be pummeled. Her look instantly darted up the rope to the pulley, and then down to the where it was tied off close to the ladder. Crouching, she climbed onto the floorboards of the loft and crawled toward the rope.

A fist landed on Silas's ear and painful ringing filled his head.

So he screamed. Even more dramatic, but he needed to keep their attention on him. "Fine, I know where she is. Just don't hurt the woman below—don't go after her—she isn't a part of this. Swear you won't and I'll tell you where Josie is."

"You don't get to make demands, maggot pie."

"I need her safe." He spit out more blood from his mouth. "Please. Just don't hurt the lady."

"We'll do what we want to her after we finish you off."
Toothless brute had straightened slightly, but he still held
his side, spittle flying as he sputtered out the words.

"Kill me and you'll never know where Josie is."

"Which is why we'll keep the lady alive—to torture
her in front of you. I'm sure you'd like that, to see her tied
down, each of us taking a poke at her." The threat on his
lips, the well-dressed man moved closer to the toothless
brute, his back directly to Georgina.

"You fucking animals." Silas twisted his body about,
one, to glance at Georgina in the shadows of the rafters
sawing at the rope with the dagger he'd given her, and two,
to see if she had cut through the rope enough that he could
snap it by writhing his weight.

He violently twisted his body about.

No luck.

His voice took on a screech. "The woman isn't a part
of this. I already told you I'll tell you where Josie is—better
yet, I'll take you to her. That way you know I won't lie
about it."

"Hmm. What ye think, boss?" The flat-faced brute
looked to the well-dressed man, then froze. "What the
hell?" His look had veered off of the well-dressed man to
Georgina in the corner.

In an instant, the man ran across the hayloft, charging
at Georgina.

She heard him charging at her before she saw him
coming, and she managed to jump back from the rope
just as he lunged at her. He crashed into the wall, just
missing her, and she screamed, her hand holding the dagger

swinging out and plunging the blade into the side of the man's neck.

The toothless brute was directly behind the first one and he snatched Georgina's arm, yanking her into his body with a blade drawn and against her neck in an instant.

Silas swung his legs out, then jerked his body as hard as he could against the rope.

The rope snapped.

In one motion, before the well-dressed man could even turn around to him, Silas slipped his bound wrists around the man's head and yanked him backward onto his chest, choking the bastard. The man struggled, arms thwapping on anything he could reach on Silas, but he couldn't gain angle, his life slipping away.

Too damn long.

For the toothless brute had Georgina in his clutches and was dragging her away from the wild flailing of the flat-faced brute with the knife in his neck. The man desperate for life—for help—but knowing he couldn't pull the knife out or he would immediately bleed to death.

Georgina wasn't screaming, but her hands were clawing on the man's arm that held the blade to her neck, trying to pull it away.

The well-dressed man's body jerked in front of Silas, but he couldn't let him go—not while there was still life in him.

"Georgina!"

Her eyes locked onto him.

"First option," Silas thundered.

It was enough of a message. Recognition sparked in her eyes.

Her hands dropped away from the brute's arm—which she was never going to beat anyway—and she set her fist into her palm, then drew her elbow up and jammed it back as hard as she could while she twisted her hips out of the way.

Solid contact on his ballocks. Enough to send the toothless man stumbling backward to the edge of the hayloft, his blade against her neck dropping away. But his hold around her chest managed to stay solid, dragging her with him.

At that moment, the flat-faced brute with the dagger in his neck yanked it out of his body.

Blood spurted and the reaction in Georgina was instant.

Her eyes rolled back in her head and she dropped, a sack of bricks.

Her sudden shift of weight against the front of the toothless brute threw his balance off and he toppled off the edge of the loft.

Georgina falling, falling, falling after him.

His future falling to her death right in front of him.

{ CHAPTER 34 }

Her eyes fluttered open, the intense pounding in her skull ripping her awake.

Pounding—so much pounding it hurt to blink. Like her head was about to explode.

A drumbeat—loud—filling her brain.

No, that wasn't a drum.

That was a heartbeat.

And why was the world around her upside down? Blurry? Why were her arms hanging by her head?

Wait, *she* was upside down.

"Georgina—Georgina—wake up—for all that is holy and good in this world, wake up."

Silas's voice.

His voice. Small and far away. But there.

She blinked again and the world around her came into focus.

She was hanging upside down in the barn she had crept into. Sawing the rope. The man attacking her. The blade into his neck. The other man grabbing her. Silas choking the third one.

"Georgina—wake up. Georgina."

An order she couldn't ignore. Her chin touched her chest as she tried to look upward to right her world.

Fabric fell in front of her face, blinding her.

"Silas?"

"Yes. Hell—yes. Georgina."

He was above her. What was in front of her? White cloth.

Her petticoat under her dress. Hanging in front of her face.

That meant…

"Silas, am I hanging upside down half naked?"

"Yes." He grunted, seething a breath as though he was dragging a thousand bricks across a field.

Her arms jerked into motion, her fingers grasping and pushing at the fabric as she tried to cover her crotch.

"I really need you to stop trying to fix your skirts and reach up to grab me."

"What?" She could feel his hands clasped around her right ankle, while her left leg was weirdly bent and angled off to the side. She shoved the fabric away from her face and looked up.

He was draped over the edge of the hayloft, his arms long and hanging down with his hands clasped around her ankle. His wrists were still bound together with the rope.

"How long have I been out?"

His face was red, the tendons along his neck popping. "Too long, and I'm stuck like this because I only have one good arm and my grip is slipping. I need you to reach out and grab the rope hanging next to your face, then pull yourself upward."

Simple directions. She could do that even through the pounding in her skull.

She reached out, grabbing the loop of the thick rope and tugging on it until she found which direction was attached to Silas. Slowly, hand over hand, she worked her way up the rope until she was bent in half, her head nearly upright. The blood started draining out of her head and the pounding eased from her brain.

"Good, now wrap your left arm around the rope multiple times so it can catch you if you lose grip."

"Why will I lose grip?" Holding herself steady with her right hand, she twisted her left forearm around the rope, again and again until she ran out of slack, then she locked her left fingers around the rope.

"Because you're going to reach out with your right hand and grab the rope between my wrists."

She nodded, quickly doing so without prodding.

He groaned, letting her right ankle drop away from his grip, and he locked his right hand around her wrist.

"I'm going to slip onto my side and swing you up. Kick out and get your foot onto the ledge."

She nodded and he rolled up onto his right side while she kicked up with her leg, her heel catching onto the top of the hayloft floor.

In the next breath, he lifted the rest of her body upward, dragging her on top of him.

Her head instantly swiveled, eyes looking for danger.

There were only two bodies lying prone in the shallow mounds of hay.

"Don't look, Georgina." Silas's fingers clasped onto her face and he drew her attention back to him.

"But I—"

"No. Don't look. You did what you had to." The blue strands in his hazel eyes pulsated, willing her to keep her

stare on him. "One is dead down below and I killed the other one. None is a sight I want you to be stuck with."

Her head shook, the weight of what had happened crushing down on her chest. "I didn't mean to. I wasn't sure I could even do anything. I don't know how I even stabbed him. I didn't think I could do it, that I was enough. I didn't think—"

His head lifted, his lips covering hers, stopping her words, her doubt. "Little dragon, you are more than enough. You are everything. You always have been. Don't ever doubt it."

She stared down at him, the world, the future in his eyes. A future she could no longer doubt, no longer question. He was it. She loved him and there would never be any other course for her.

She nodded. "I won't. And I love you. I never told you and I should have, but to speak it—" Her words choked off, her head shaking. She swallowed hard. "My heart has led me to foolish places before."

"This isn't foolish." He shifted his still-bound wrists up, then slipped his arms around her head. "It isn't wrong. It's real—more real than anything I've ever known before."

"My heart knew it long ago."

A smile transformed his face, so brilliant it sent her heart into a manic flurry. "I'm glad the rest of you followed." He dragged her down for another kiss, then let his head clunk onto the boards of the hayloft. "And now that you've acquainted yourself with your dagger, I would appreciate some help cutting out of these ropes." He shifted his bound wrists upward and away from her head.

She laughed, pushing herself up off the wide mass of him, her hands slipping into the interior of his coat to search for one of his hidden daggers. "That, I know I can manage."

{ CHAPTER 35 }

"I cannot believe you woke the man and his wife up."
Georgina sank onto the side of the bed at the coaching inn,
pulling her right leg up to unlace her boot.

"I'm sure he's accustomed to it." Silas had cleaned off
most of the blood on his face at the blacksmith's, enough
for the time being, at least. Watching her, he dragged off his
own boots, his coat, waistcoat, and lawn shirt, leaving them
where they fell for he had more important things to attend
to. Namely, his wife.

He went over to her as she pulled free her right boot
and he picked up her left calf and worked the laces to
remove her remaining boot. "I imagine he gets couples
wanting to marry at all times of the night."

With her leg high in the air as he pulled free her boot
and dragged off her stocking, she leaned back on the bed,
balancing on her propped elbows. "With bridegrooms
that use the anvil as leverage to set their own dislocated
shoulders back into place before the ceremony?"

Dropping her boot and stocking, he crawled over her
on the bed, locking his legs on the outside of her body and
curling down over her. "I'm sure the many bridegrooms he's
seen come into his shop are in all manners of disarray—
blood seeping out, mud splattered, shoulders out of sockets.
I'm sure it runs the gamut of injury and mayhem in his
business."

She stared up at him, the smile on her face as heated as a blacksmith's forge. "The grumpy look souring his face told me otherwise."

"Yet we did not bother him for long. It was the quickest of ceremonies—I paid him extra for that—so I imagine he was back in bed before we even made it five steps from his door." He nuzzled into her neck, his fingers slipping under her to work down the row of buttons along her spine as his lips chased her skin. "Which was good because all I have wanted—needed—since I saw you disappear over the edge of that loft has been to get your body naked under mine."

It was true. He needed this. Needed to feel her from the inside out, deep and raw and screaming his name. Proving to him that she was alive and safe and in his arms. Proving she hadn't died on him.

He almost didn't veer straight to the blacksmith's shop after getting out of that barn because he needed her with the force of a thousand suns, but she needed the wedding and he saw it on her face.

She needed the wedding to know this was real and he would be hers forever.

And to make her happy, he would give her anything.

Plus, he was more than done with the journey. He wanted the damn destination.

He wanted the rest of his life with her.

Her hands wrapped around his neck and she laughed that breathless chuckle that cut into his heart every time he heard it. "Then rip the damn dress."

Her words weren't fully out and he had the fabric gripped in his fingers, ripping it apart, tearing the whole of it off her body like he was a rabid animal.

She didn't let him have all the fun, her fingers popping buttons as she tore open the fall front of his trousers and shoved them down his legs.

A flurry of clothing and seams ripping until he had her naked body recaptured on the bed, hovering above her, staring at her flushed face.

As much as he needed to drive his cock into her, he paused, taking the moment to believe it, to believe that this was his life.

Georgina looking up at him with awe and fire and wanton love in her eyes. Looking up at him as though he was her world.

She sure as hell was his.

Holding himself up on his right arm propped on the bed, he dragged his left fingers down her body, taking in every curve, holding the heft of her right breast in his palm as he toyed with her nipple, ripening it. His fingers went down along her waist and out along her hip. He dipped farther down the outside of her thigh, only so that he could veer inward and drag his fingertips upward along her inner thigh.

There. That spot. Midway up her thigh and her leg twitched, needing to escape the tickle, but refusing to do so for how good it felt.

He loved that spot on her. Loved teasing it. Loved testing her mettle with it. Loved licking it. Loved the taste of it. Loved everything about it.

She lifted her mouth to his chest, her tongue making circles across his skin, the soft sound of it deeply carnal.

"Why do you do this to me?" She said into his skin.

"What?"

"Drive my body into madness before you take me into bliss."

His chest shook in a laugh. "The madder your body is the harder I get to take you."

Her lips pulled away from his skin and her eyes found his. The look in the blue pure wanton. "You can take me now. As hard as you want. Whatever you want."

He groaned. Heaven help him. The raging emotion in his chest was going to kill him one of these days while pleasuring her.

He ran his hand up her thigh, slipping into her folds. She wasn't lying, she was flush, wet and ready for him.

"You're going to be the death of me."

"Or the life of you."

That, she was. The only life he wanted from here on.

In one thrust, he drove into her, filling her to the hilt.

An instant scream of pleasure, his name on her lips.

He drew out, then slid in harder, her body taking the blow. Again and again and again. Her leg wrapped up and around him, her heel in his back, prodding him on with every plunge. He could feel her inner walls starting to tighten.

Too early, but he'd take it as the first round.

He continued pumping her, long heavy strokes until her back arched, her body crushing into him.

He didn't stop, made her ride out the orgasm on the
slide of his cock going in and out. Her gasps yielded and he
pulled out and lifted her waist, flipping her over on the bed.

Her breathless chuckle came into the air as she went on
all fours. "More?"

"Always more."

He knocked her knees outward with his legs and set his
shaft at her slit, his hands running along the globes of her
buttocks, pressing into the muscles. Gripping onto her hip
bones, he slammed into her and the moans coming from
her nearly undid him.

He reached around, sliding his fingers into her folds,
circling the nub that was already hard and quivering under
his touch. Drawing her into her next orgasm, even though
he could feel the tremble in her legs. She didn't think she
could go there.

He knew she could.

"It's going to happen, little dragon."

Words not possible, she nodded, screaming as his cock
set a harrowing pace that he matched with his hand.

Control quickly leaving him, he growled. "Come for
me. Now."

It was all it took and her body bucked, her head
throwing back in a scream as she writhed against him, the
orgasm taking hold of her body from head to toe.

The clench around his shaft so intense, he couldn't
slide out, only drill deeper, reaching a depth in her he never
knew before he ripped apart into a thousand sparks, losing
time and place.

He collapsed downward, dragging her down with him and clasping her against the length of him as he hit the bed. Her body landed on top of him, as limp as his own muscles felt.

He'd hoped to draw a third one out of her before he broke. But there'd be time for that in a few minutes. And then a few minutes after that, and a few minutes after that.

All the time in the world.

His breath still heaving, he absent-mindedly traced the crescent moon birthmark on her lower back with his thumb. He loved that mark. He'd discovered it days ago while his tongue was taking a tour of her body. The shape of it, the oddity of the placement, it reminded him that she was flesh and blood, just like him.

That he would be capable of making her happy. Of making her his.

This. This was the rest of his life. By the grace of the fates, somehow, this was it.

He didn't deserve it. But there was no tearing her away from him now.

He looked down at her upturned face and his finger lifted to trace across a line that had popped up in the middle of her forehead. "Worry has crept onto your face. I don't think I have ravaged you sufficiently if doubts are already crowding into your head."

She half smiled. "No, it has nothing to do with this—with us. On that accord I have no doubts."

"Then what is it?"

"Willow. And also, those men—what did they want?"

"You didn't hear?"

She shook her head.

"They wanted to know where Josie was."

Her head popped up, her jaw hanging open. "What?"

"Her father sent them. Somehow, he finally connected the current me to who I was at his estate."

"He doesn't know Josie died?"

He shook his head. "No. Once he returned to England, he was never able to find her—mostly because she was always on jobs for the Guardians—jobs like yours—that set her on the skirts of ballrooms and operas. Places her father would never think to look for her."

"He's a monster."

Silas sighed. "The worst of them."

Her mouth closed, a frown bringing down her face. "Are you…"

"Going to take care of him?"

She nodded.

He looked up at the canopy of the four-post bed, his eyes tracing the scrolling leaves in the weave of the dark blue fabric. "For some reason I never understood, Josie never wanted me to kill him. Her hatred for him was vicious, but she would never let me send him into the ground."

A long sigh left him and he looked to Georgina. "But this—what happened—he sent men that would have killed you. And that won't stand."

She stared at him for a long moment, then gave him the slightest nod. No arguments. No reasons for peace. No pleas for mercy. She wanted the man wiped from this earth just as much as he did.

His little dragon, always surprising him.

He twisted a long lock of her hair around his forefinger. "And your worry on your sister?"

"I am afraid what we will find when we get back to London. What has happened to her."

He started to open his mouth, then closed it. Secrets better kept to himself.

Except no.

Honesty.

He'd intended honesty.

He shifted under her, but then set his hand along the small of her back, keeping her in place atop him. "I found out something a while ago that you may or may not want to know."

Her eyes went wide. "About Willow? What?"

"I haven't told you because I didn't want to give you false hope."

"I will take any hope, false or not."

His lips pursed for a moment, unsure about continuing for the hope that was already shining bright in her eyes. Hope he didn't want to stoke. "When I went back to Toften Hall, and then to London while I had you locked at Yarstone, I did some investigating—or rather, I mentioned to the right person that I was curious about Mr. Thatcher."

"Mr. Thatcher—why?"

"I was curious what his business was—I know he owns the Alabaster gaming hall, but what I really wanted to know was what his chances were at retrieving Willow safely from wherever she had been taken by Lord Fugal."

"And?" Her fingers curled into his chest.

"Mr. Thatcher just happens to be a guardian—or was one."

Her head snapped back, her eyes blinking hard. "He's a guardian? Like you? How did you not know this?"

"I don't know most of the guardians. It is safer for all of us if we don't know about each other, save for a few trusted cohorts."

"Wait—but you said once a guardian, always a guardian. Does that mean he is still a guardian?"

"I can only assume, in some fashion, he is. What I do know, is that if he did manage to find Willow, his chances at bringing her home safely are innumerably better than they were before I knew that fact."

She exhaled, her face relaxing.

Too much hope that he didn't want to see destroyed if her sister had not survived her ordeal.

"But it is not a guarantee. That is why I didn't want to tell you."

She nodded, the wrinkle reappearing on her forehead. "Then we need to get back to London to see if we are needed in any way."

"We'll leave tomorrow." His hand buried into the back of her hair. "The fastest route, as long as your nights are mine."

"All my nights are yours." Her head bowed down, her lips pressing against his chest for a long breath. She looked up at him. "Thank you for telling me. For trusting me with that information."

"No more lies. You get the full of me now, Georgina." He met her stare, drowning in the light blue depths that

had once looked at him so coldly, but now seared him from the inside out.

A life he never thought possible, stemming from the wonder of those eyes.

She smiled. "The full of you is all I ever needed."

{ EPILOGUE }

"I wanted in on it." Georgina looked over at him from her perch on one of the wingback chairs by the fireplace, her lips twisted into sourness.

"Damn, what have I created?" Silas walked into the study in their London townhouse. He'd hoped to find her waiting for him naked in bed. Yet that was not to be with his wife. At least not in this instance.

Not when he'd sneaked out of the house earlier while it was still daylight, and now it was only hours from dawn.

He stopped in front of her. "When did you grow a tongue for blood?"

"Just one man's blood. And that happened the moment you told me about what he did to Josie. And it was solidified when he tried to have you killed. Me as well."

"All fine points." He dropped his leather saddlebag on the floor and the knives inside clanked into each other.

She glanced down to it. "What do you have in that bag?"

"Lots of steel." He shrugged. "Overkill for the job, but better to be prepared. I have too much on the line now to go anywhere unprepared."

He shuffled forward and set his hands on the armrests of the chair, trapping her as he leaned down and kissed her lips that were still puffy from his ravaging hours ago.

"Is it done? Tell me that bastard is rotting in hell."

He hid a smirk as he pulled up. He couldn't fault her for her bloodlust. But he also didn't want to encourage it.

One killer in the family was more than enough.

"It is."

"And you are not injured?"

"No."

"Did Callum go with you?"

"He did."

"Is he fine?"

"He is."

She hissed out a dramatic sigh, her glare going on him. "You said you would tell me when you were leaving to do it."

"I lied." In all honesty, he never would have told her when he was going after Josie's father. He didn't want her anywhere near that bastard, no matter how much training he'd given her during the last months or how good she currently was with a blade.

And she *was* good.

But he was never going to let the air of that dung heap taint his wife's skin.

Her arms clasped together just below her breasts, her eyes narrowed at him. "I hate your lies."

"Intentions have limitations. The only lies I tell you are important ones." He reached down and wiggled his fingers behind her arms, grabbing them to pull her up onto her feet and drag her into his arms. She only resisted slightly, not actually enough to stop his motions. "And this was an important one. I wasn't about to have you in danger." His hand dropped down in between them to caress the hard bump in her lower belly. "Or this one in danger."

Her jaw dropped as she exhaled slightly, her eyes rolling to the ceiling. "Then that, I have to concede…was an acceptable lie."

"I thought as much."

Her look sank down to him. "You still could have told me where you were going. You would have been able to convince me to stay here."

"Would I have?"

She grinned. "Of course."

His brow furrowed at her.

She groaned a sigh. "Of course, I would have stayed home. I am no more going to put this babe at risk than you are." Her hands slipped under his arms and around his torso. "I should have known some scheme was afoot the second Daphne showed up. She said she was bored, and I've never once seen that woman bored."

In a turn he hadn't seen coming, Georgina and Daphne had become fast friends once he had managed to stick them into a room together. It had happened on a balmy night in a supper-box at Vauxhall Gardens, and probably had much to do with the punch that had been served during dinner. Silas had stepped out into the gardens to talk to an acquaintance and on his way back to the box, he'd distinctly heard them laughing—real, gut-straining laughter. Laughter that had ceased the moment he'd stepped into the box, so he could only imagine it had been about him.

It didn't matter. Anything to bond them. He trusted Daphne unequivocally. And now Georgina did too.

Callum on the opposite end, still hadn't quite forgiven Georgina for her escape. His ego matched the size of him and she had bruised it fairly deep. But he was warming to her.

"I did ask Daphne to stop by." He pressed her lower back closer to him, his need to have her body next to his never abating. "What did you two do tonight?"

"She fleeced me out of all the coin I could find in the study playing piquet."

He laughed. One never gambled with Daphne. There was only one way that would ever turn out. "Did you start out winning?"

"Yes."

He laughed again. "How many games in did you start losing?"

Her head tilted back as she counted in her mind. "Seven—no eight."

Lucky eight. "That sounds exactly true to form with her."

Georgina's lips pursed. "I don't plan on giving up that easily with her. I only started playing the game this year. I'll best her yet."

"I imagine you will, little dragon."

He leaned down, his lips meeting her neck. "Can I bring you upstairs and get you naked now?"

Her face turned toward him, her lips wisping across his cheek. "Who says we need to go upstairs?"

He laughed. His wife, always ready for the adventure, always surprising him.

He wouldn't have it any other way.

And now he couldn't even imagine a life without her, she had become that vital to his soul, to his breath, to his beating heart.

A gift from the past, from Josie, that had led him to a future that completed him.

{ Bonus Epilogue }

Her breath gone, Georgina grabbed Willow's forearm with her left fingers, squeezing it. Her nails dug into her sister's skin, but she couldn't help it, not for how much pain was rolling through her body.

After a moment—too long of a moment—the pain subsided enough to breathe.

She looked up at Willow, blowing a wet strand of hair out of her face. "Thank Jack for me."

Willow's eyebrows drew together. "Thank him for what?"

"For dragging Silas out of here. It was smart of you to get Jack to do it. He wasn't listening to us and I was afraid my husband was going to be sick."

"*I* was afraid he was going to be sick." Willow chuckled, her hand wrapping around Georgina's grip on her arm and trying to ease the nails from digging in farther. "He's been listening to you screaming in agony for the last eight hours. It's only by sheer will that he hasn't already retched. It's sweet, actually. He cannot stand you in pain."

"I cannot stand me in pain. I"—a scream ripped out of her throat as a fresh gush of pain ripped her body in two. Her fingernails redigging into Willow's arm, her body curled over as the wretched scream petered out.

She pushed down on the sheet across her belly that was soaked with her sweat. She needed air. More air. More than the open window was allowing.

She caught her breath, her stare locked on the mound of skin protruding out from her body that was suddenly the bane of her existence. For months she'd carried this babe around with the utmost care, and now it thought to turn on her like this? She sucked in a breath between clenched teeth. "Talk to me—talk to me about anything other than this pain."

"Can I talk to you about the blood you're drawing on my arm?"

"No. No talking about it. No showing me. Talk about something else."

Willow looked up from Georgina on the bed, her gaze scanning the bedroom she and Silas shared. "Ahh, I like our new room. It's now just as nice as this one."

"Yes? Really?" Georgina somehow managed a smile. "Better than the last time you were here?"

"It is incredibly cozy, but still elegant. I never thought you could have turned this pile of stones into what it has become, but you have. The main drawing room, the library, and the dining hall, all of them gorgeous."

That made her smile. "And just in time for Auntie and Uncle to visit."

"Exactly. They'll never know what this place looked like before." Willow patted her hand that was still clutching her arm. "And you can give all the credit to Silas so that Uncle will finally forgive him."

Georgina cringed. "Are there still undertones of irritation in his voice when he talks of Silas?"

"I don't know that he'll ever forgive the elopement. Mine was reasonable in his mind, while yours was not."

Willow shrugged. "But he also sees how much Silas adores you, so his ire is waning. Besides, Silas had Auntie under his spell after the first week you were back in London, so she's working on Uncle as well."

Another surge of pain gripped Georgina, the most brutal one yet. A scream turned into a groan then turned into words. "I don't want this. I want to keep it inside. Just for a while longer."

Willow dropped her face close to hers. "You have no choice, Georgie. It is coming whether you're ready or not." Her fingers pushed the hair out of Georgina's face.

The midwife ducked down between her legs, then popped up. "The babe is ready to come—it is time to push again, m'lady. Hard this time."

For as long and as brutal as the labor had dragged on throughout the day, the actual birth was a relief.

Five agonizing pushes, complete with bone-shattering screams, and the babe was out.

The relief of that one moment was interrupted by Silas charging into the room.

"Did I miss it?" His eyes on his wife, the pain of worry in his voice was unmistakable.

The babe squawked a cry.

She shook her head. "No. You're here for its first cry. You didn't miss anything."

Silas looked to the midwife.

The midwife held the babe, slippery and naked, up to Silas. "'Tis a girl, m'lord."

She bundled the babe and moved to hand the girl to Georgina.

Her hands shaking, Georgina reached out, taking her babe, clutching her to her chest as she wiped the streaks of blood from her face.

Silas had moved next to the bed, dropping onto his knees, his left hand going to cradle the back of Georgina's head while his right cradled the back of the babe's head. His words came out rough, like he'd been the one screaming for the past day. "The blood—are you going to be sick?"

She shook her head. "No—I'm going to be happy."

This babe in her arms, this tiny being with her face scrunched and angry and giving spurts of little cries—it was everything. It had haunted her for months, whether her past would interfere with her future. Whether what had happened with Leroy's babe would happen again. A worry that she never spoke out loud, for fear that putting the words to sound would make it a reality.

But it wasn't.

This was the reality.

This child. This man next to her with tears brimming in his hazel eyes and a torrent of love for their child already unmistakable.

Willow sighed and stood from her chair at the opposite side of the bed. She leaned down to kiss Georgina on her sweaty brow. "Thanks for going first, Georgie. You did well. Even if you did scare me half to Hades and back."

Georgina reached out and brushed at the smeared blood on her sister's arm. "Sorry about your arm."

Willow grinned. "Don't worry, I imagine you will be my pin cushion in another two months." She waddled out of the room, holding her lower back for stability for her own babe was due soon.

Georgina set the babe to her breast, and her girl was quick to latch on, hungry after her own ordeal. They waited in silence until the midwife finished and left the room.

It took Silas several more long breaths before he clasped his forehead down onto the side of her face, his voice ragged. "I never even imagined that this could be mine—you, the babe. But it is the world. My world. You are everything, my little dragon." His head tilted, his gaze going to the top of the babe's head. "And you are everything beyond everything, my even littler dragon."

Georgina's heart swelled in that instant, so hard and painful that it took her breath away, but in a way that only made her grateful to be alive.

She reached up, her fingers settling on the side of his face. "And you are ours."

~ About the Author ~

K.J. Jackson is the *USA Today* bestselling author of the
*Hold Your Breath, Lords of Fate, Lords of Action,
Revelry's Tempest, Valor of Vinehill, Box of Draupnir,
Exile, Guardians of the Bones,* and *Flame Moon* series.

She specializes in historical and paranormal romance,
loves to travel (road trips are the best!), and is a sucker for a
good story in any genre. She lives in Minnesota with
her husband, two children, and a dog who
has taken the sport of bed-hogging
to new heights.

Visit her at www.kjjackson.com

~ Author's Note ~

Thank you for allowing my stories into your life and time—
it is an honor!

Be sure to check out all my historical romances
(each is a stand-alone story):

Never miss a new release or sale!
Be sure to sign up for my VIP Email List at
www.KJJackson.com

Connect with me!
www.KJJackson.com ~or~ kjk19jackson@gmail.com

Made in the USA
Las Vegas, NV
28 February 2024